Shadow headed s
and shoved his n
while Ben approached Jamie. "It's okay. I'm here."

"Where did he go?"

"Who? What did you see?"

"A—a man."

"Up here? That's impossible."

Jamie pushed herself into a sitting position and pointed. "Oh, yeah? Tell that to your dog."

Ben realized she was right. Shadow had stayed at the window, growling and pawing at the sill.

Rocky Mountain K-9 Unit

These police officers fight for justice
with the help of their brave canine partners.

Detection Detail by Terri Reed, April 2022
Ready to Protect by Valerie Hansen, May 2022
Hiding in Montana by Laura Scott, June 2022
Undercover Assignment by Dana Mentink, July 2022
Defending from Danger by Jodie Bailey, August 2022
Tracking a Killer by Elizabeth Goddard, September 2022
Explosive Revenge by Maggie K. Black, October 2022
Rescue Mission by Lynette Eason, November 2022
Christmas K-9 Unit Heroes by Lenora Worth and Katy Lee, December 2022

Valerie Hansen was thirty when she awoke to the presence of the Lord in her life and turned to Jesus. She now lives in a renovated farmhouse on the breathtakingly beautiful Ozark Plateau of Arkansas and is privileged to share her personal faith by telling the stories of her heart for Love Inspired. Life doesn't get much better than that!

READY TO PROTECT

VALERIE HANSEN

LOVE INSPIRED SUSPENSE
INSPIRATIONAL ROMANCE

Special thanks and acknowledgment are given to Valerie Hansen
for her contribution to the Rocky Mountain K-9 Unit miniseries.

LOVE INSPIRED® SUSPENSE

INSPIRATIONAL ROMANCE

Recycling programs
for this product may
not exist in your area.

ISBN-13: 978-1-335-72305-5

Ready to Protect

Love Inspired
22 Adelaide St. West, 41st Floor
Toronto, Ontario M5H 4E3, Canada
www.LoveInspired.com

Printed in U.S.A.

Before I formed thee in the belly I knew thee.
—*Jeremiah* 1:5

I started to list the friends and colleagues who are special to me and discovered that the list was too long, so I'll thank the Lord for all of them and for the opportunities He has given me and continues to offer. I never cease to be amazed and blessed.

ONE

Jamie London was so afraid she was trembling inside. She'd been on edge ever since witnessing a murder several months ago, but this was different. Worse. Her level of anxiety was climbing off the charts. She didn't want to be in busy Denver. She didn't want to be interrogated by the FBI. And she certainly didn't want to be noticed or recognized. Not now. *Especially* not now. The sooner she could escape the imposing government offices the better. She just wished the agent in charge hadn't ordered her to park in the dimly lit garage instead of on the street.

The elevator taking her back to tier three of the concrete parking structure halted with a slight jerk. Doors whooshed open. Eyes widening, she peered out into the gloom. Traffic on the busy streets outside hummed in the background like a hive of angry bees, but up there where she felt so isolated nothing moved.

There were no suspicious footsteps, no dark

figures loitering in the shadows, no sounds that should have triggered foreboding. And yet she was so scared she could barely convince herself to take the first steps toward her car.

"We'll make it," Jamie said, tenderly patting her stomach and believing that the unborn baby nestled beneath her heart could hear and understand. Pulling her hobo bag to the front, she held it like a shield and left the elevator.

FBI Special Agent in Charge Michael Bridges had offered to summon someone to escort her to her car after her interview, but she had declined rather than wait around. All she'd wanted was to get out of there ASAP. To escape the building as well as the tragic memories his questions had dredged up. Being the key witness to Congresswoman Natasha Clark's murder was not something Jamie could deny. Testifying was her civic duty. But she wished she could leave that part of her life as far behind her as she had her unfaithful husband.

"It's not your fault, honey," she cooed to the baby. "You can't help who your daddy was, can you? Of course not."

Speaking aloud calmed Jamie some. She truly was not alone. Not anymore. She and her little girl would stick together no matter what, and she'd do her very best to assume the roles of both parents. Lots of women did it. She could, too.

Her jacket didn't quite meet in the front anymore, but most of the time it kept her warm enough for early May weather in Denver. Tights beneath her tunic helped, too, yet she shivered in the gloom.

Sounds of her own footsteps echoed down the aisle of the designated visitor area as she hurried to her car, unlocking it with her electronic key. Someone had pulled too close to the driver's door so she tossed the bulky purse in ahead of her, turned sideways and started to squeeze through the narrow opening. Seven months' worth of baby didn't hamper her most of the time but in this case, it was a tight fit.

Jamie held her breath as she strained to wiggle into the car. Silence surrounded her. The rapid beat of her heart echoed in her ears. A car door slammed in the distance. Jamie froze. Tried to listen past the thudding of her pulse, the raggedness of her breathing.

The baby kicked, startling her and providing enough extra incentive to propel her the rest of the way in. Her hip hit the steering wheel and glanced off. *Ouch!* She pushed against the wheel in order to drag her left leg the rest of the way and slam the door. *The key?* Where was the ignition key? She'd just had it in her hand.

Had she dropped it when she'd been struggling with the door? Or was it back in her purse?

Muttering, "Key, key, key…" she patted the seat and slipped her fingers into the crack between it and the center console. Nothing.

Her shoulder bag had slid to the floor on the passenger side when she'd thrown it in ahead of her. She reached to the right. Her fingertips brushed the strap. Almost had it. Almost, but not quite.

Frustrated and sensing impending trouble, despite the comfort of her car, Jamie leaned to stretch farther.

A boom with a whine split the silence. Hurt her ears. The car's windshield shattered into a spiderweb of shards, held in place only by the layer of plastic laminated between two sheets of glass for safety.

Jamie may have screamed. She wasn't sure. What she did hear almost before the echo of the attack had died down was the wail of alarms and an automated voice instructing everyone to shelter in place. *Well, duh*, she thought. *Like I'm going anywhere now.*

More shots reverberated through the tiers of the garage, this time with more bang and less whine. Tires were squealing. A motor raced.

Jamie pressed herself to the seat until the sounds of immediate danger ceased, then slowly raised on one elbow, trying to keep her head below the level of the dashboard.

Running feet pounded down stairways and elevators slid open. In minutes, armed men and women had deployed up and down the aisles and around her damaged car.

She recognized SAC Bridges as he shouted orders and reached for her driver's door with his free hand while the other pointed a lethal-looking handgun at the ceiling.

"Are you hurt?" he yelled.

"I… I don't think so." Jamie opened the door slightly. "What happened?"

"Looks like you were shot at. Did you see the shooter? Can you identify the driver of the black SUV?"

"I didn't see a soul."

"Okay. We should be able to get info from our security cameras." Bridges motioned to one of the nearby plainclothes officers wearing a plastic ID badge. "Stay with her until the ambulance gets here and make sure she doesn't move until we're sure she isn't injured."

"Yes, sir," the dark-haired agent said.

Jamie didn't argue. She didn't have it left in her at the moment. Lying on her right shoulder she closed her eyes and caressed her baby bump with her left hand, apologizing to her child over and over. "Mommy's so sorry, little one. So, so sorry."

Had pregnancy enhanced her senses? she wondered. Was that why she'd felt frightened even before the attack? Or was the fear simply a result of having to relive the congresswoman's last moments for the FBI?

"It doesn't matter," she whispered. Bile rose in her throat. Her whole body was trembling. Reality settled in her heart and filled her mind with thanksgiving. If she hadn't dropped the key and leaned down to retrieve her purse, the bullet might have injured her. Or worse.

There was only one suitable reaction to that horrifying conclusion. Keeping her eyes squeezed shut she turned her thoughts and words toward heaven with a fervent "Thank You, Father. Thank You, Jesus" punctuated by silent tears of gratitude.

Five hours away, in the Wyoming foothills of the Bighorn Mountains, Ben Sawyer wasn't as antsy about being officially sidelined as he might have been if the injury had been his rather than that of his K-9 partner, Shadow. The big black Doberman had been strong and healthy until an accident during training at the Rocky Mountain K-9 Unit headquarters in Denver had left him limping. Somehow, a gun fired during the exercise didn't contain the standard blanks, and Shadow had been startled and landed badly. With plenty to keep Ben occupied on the vast ranch he and his father, Drew, operated, he didn't mind being sidelined for a short time.

As long as this hiatus doesn't last too long, Ben told himself. The sooner Shadow was cleared to return to duty, the happier they'd both be.

He ran his fingertips and thumb down his scruffy cheeks to meet at the cleft in his chin. It was nice to not have to shave daily while he was working on the ranch. And these well-worn clothes suited him far more than those he was expected to wear as a K-9 officer, too, although the badge, lanyard and Kevlar vest his unit used were better than having to adopt matching Colorado police uniforms. His allegiance was, after all, pledged to Wyoming first. The RMK-9 Unit was a relatively new mobile team comprised of handlers and their canine partners. They were under contract to the FBI and served the entire Rocky Mountain Region. Ben had been recruited from the local PD by his former military leader, who headed the unit.

The cell phone clipped to his belt vibrated. Shadow alerted despite the muted sound, his ears raised to a point and attention focusing on his human partner. Ben smiled. "Take it easy, boy. I don't think this is about work. You haven't been okayed for active duty yet."

Noting the caller's name and number, however, Ben was puzzled. It was Tyson Wilkes, his friend and boss.

"Sawyer," Ben said. "What's up?"

"I have a job for you."

"A job? I just told Shadow it was too soon. He's going to think I fibbed." Ben smiled at his K-9 partner as though the dog was capable of getting the joke.

"I'm not asking you to come back to Denver," Tyson said. "I'm sending you a witness to protect."

"Me? Here?"

"Yes, you. I know it sounds odd but she's a special case. We suspect there has already been at least one attempt to silence her and she's refusing to shelter in Denver."

Ben blew a sigh. "So, arrest her and keep her in protective custody."

"Not that easy, I'm afraid. Since the incident with Shadow at the training center indicated an internal problem and the fact that this murder witness was ambushed in our parking garage, I'm hesitant to keep her within a system that might be compromised at present."

Scowling, Ben cupped the phone more tightly. "What are you *not* telling me?"

"I'm getting to that. We've been investigating the training mishap in-house. A wire to the alarm system on the armory room had been tampered with and we suspect that somebody on the inside got in and replaced the normal blank cartridges of the gun with a homemade version that was intended to cause real harm. That's likely what rattled the rookie during the training exercise and inadvertently caused the hip injury to your dog. We're just fortunate nobody was actually shot. Including your Shadow."

"When could anyone have done all that tampering without being seen?"

"We don't know. Naturally there were no prints and it looks like whatever tools were used came from right here."

"Terrific."

"Yeah. So, getting back to business, do you want to drive down and pick up the witness I mentioned, or shall I just send her to you?"

Ben rolled his eyes and sighed again. "I suppose it makes more sense to send her. Otherwise I'll be facing a ten-hour round trip."

"Okay. As soon as the medics give her a clean bill of health, I'll get someone from the local PD to chauffer her to your place. I assume there's plenty of room?"

"I'll arrange to give her the whole loft and move my office downstairs for a week or so. I hope this assignment isn't going to take a lot longer than that."

"Trial is set for the end of the month. Can you last three weeks?"

"I'll manage. My dad hasn't been himself lately so I won't mind spending a little more time with him. Mrs. Edgerton comes every day to cook for us and I can increase her hours, too. Just keep me posted, will you? I want to know what Forensics learns about that dummy ammo."

"So do I," Tyson told him. "Hang in there, buddy. Sorry I can't give you hazardous-duty pay for this job like we used to get in the army."

"I'll manage. Anything else?"

"Not off the top of my head. Keep in touch."

"Right. Bye." Ben didn't see any reason to remind his old friend and current boss that the Double S cattle ranch provided a more than adequate income. He hadn't entered law enforcement for the pay; he did it because it was right, something he'd learned years ago serving as an army ranger with Tyson and several of the others who had been recruited for the Rocky Mountain K-9 Unit—men like Nelson and Lucas. They were good guys, good handlers and, for Tyson's sake, Ben hoped the team he'd assembled would pass their year's probationary period and be made permanent.

"Shadow, stay," Ben commanded as he headed for the stairs.

Clearly disappointed, the Doberman laid his chin on his front paws and gave Ben such a sad look he was tempted to rescind the order. "Maybe tomorrow, boy. The vet said to keep you from using that sore hip for at least one more day. Climbing stairs isn't good for you."

The mournful expression on Shadow's face made Ben laugh and extend a hand. "All right. But take it slow, okay? We want you healed and back to work as soon as our babysitting job is over."

Panting and trying to wag his almost nonexistent tail, the sleek, well-muscled dog took three measured steps at Ben's side, then broke and leaped up the stairs to the loft, bridging two and three at a time. When he reached the top he wheeled and looked down at his favorite human while giving a perfect canine imitation of a big grin.

Ben had to laugh. "Guess you're feeling fine, huh?"

Shadow barked once, his tongue lolling, his whole body quivering with excitement.

A voice called from the direction of the kitchen. "Everything okay out there?"

"Fine, Dad," Ben shouted back. "Just fixing the loft for company. When Mrs. E. gets here, tell her we'll have an extra mouth to feed for the next few weeks. I'll fill her in later."

Drew Sawyer stuck his head through the doorway. "You're not giving up your office, are you?"

"Only temporarily. Our visitor is work related, and I want her to be comfortable, and the loft is like a separate apartment."

Besides, that will keep her out of our hair. Looking down on his dad from the second story, Ben thought Drew looked even older than his sixty-plus years. Truth to tell, he hadn't seemed like himself since finding out he had an older son who'd been kept a secret from him all these decades and Christopher Fuller's continuing refusal to speak to the father he had never known.

Ben had done all he could to bring them together, but nothing had helped. Drew's depression was another reason why Ben didn't mind spending more time at the ranch. He might not be able to reunite Drew with his estranged son, but he could at least demonstrate his own devotion to the man and their ranch. That had to count for something.

* * *

The car trip would have been more tedious for Jamie if she hadn't dozed off almost immediately. That was another drawback she'd discovered with pregnancy. She was tired all the time and had started actually taking naps. The whole premise of sleeping in the middle of the day rankled her, but she was willing to do whatever was necessary to nurture her unborn daughter.

Skylar Morgan, the Denver police detective at the wheel of the unmarked car, smiled over at her. "Good morning. Sleep well?"

Jamie yawned and stretched. "Unfortunately." Looking out the window at the passing terrain, she asked, "What did I miss?"

Skylar chuckled. "All of Colorado north of Denver and half of Wyoming. We're almost to the Double S."

"Okay." Jamie yawned again. "How did you manage to draw this duty? Is somebody mad at you?"

Another light laugh. "Naw. You scare all the guys." She eyed Jamie's baby bump. "When are you due?"

"Not soon enough," Jamie quipped. "I'm more than ready to sleep on my stomach again and put this baby to bed in a crib."

"I get that. Boy or girl?"

"Girl."

"Have you chosen a name?"

"No." Jamie shook her head. "This pregnancy was not planned, and I'm still having trouble wrapping my mind around reality."

"What does your husband say?"

Jamie gritted her teeth and took a settling breath before answering. "Greg is my ex-husband. I'd just as soon he didn't even know I'm expecting."

"Doesn't he have a father's right to know? I mean, won't he be angry if he finds out another way?"

"Greg is always angry about something," Jamie said. Her nostrils flared. "The night I told him I was pursuing divorce he spent hours convincing me I should reconsider. Then, after I gave in to him and actually thought he was going to try to change, he laughed at me like it was a big joke. That really hurt."

"I'm so sorry."

"I was, too, at first," Jamie said. "But then I realized that the best thing for me and my baby was getting Greg out of our lives for good. I trusted him and he betrayed me—in more ways than one."

"Was *he* behind the shooting in the FBI garage today? I got the impression it had to do with your witnessing a murder."

"I'm sure it was either that or random," Jamie agreed. "I haven't heard a peep out of Greg since he signed the divorce papers so I imagine he's moved on to one of his girlfriends and forgotten about me."

"From your lips to God's ears," Skylar said, her words being drowned out by the announcement of the GPS. "Destination on your right, three hundred feet."

Jamie leaned forward slightly and peered into the distance. All she could see was an archway and gray scrub dotting the uneven terrain.

"Where's the ranch?"

"Right here," the detective said as she slowed and wheeled through the open metal gate. "I haven't been out here before, but Sergeant Wilkes described the place. It's apparently huge."

"I guess it must be. Where's the house, *Montana*?"

"Nearly." Skylar had been smiling. Now, she sobered. "Are you sure you're going to be okay way out here in the middle of nowhere? What if you go into labor?"

"I have at least six more weeks," Jamie explained.

"Okay. Have it your way."

"If I had it my way I'd be back in my apartment in Denver, editing the last wildlife photos I took and submitting them for publication."

She bent with difficulty to reach into a bag at her feet and withdraw an expensive camera.

"Wow. Looks like you can do just about anything with that. Will it fly?"

"Nope. Doesn't wash windows, either, but it does do a lot of great stuff." As the car slowed in front of a rambling log home, she rolled down her window and pointed the top-of-the-line camera at individuals standing on the covered porch.

Focusing, Jamie was able to see more clearly than she could with the naked eye and the sight stole her breath. The brim of a black Stetson shaded a man's eyes and the dark shadow of a fledgling beard made his cheeks and chin stand out against the light plaid of his Western shirt. A rodeo belt buckle accented his trim waist above well-fitting but worn jeans. Western leather boots with slightly turned-up toes supported a strong, athletic figure.

Her finger clicked the shutter automatically in a series of shots that changed with every foot the car traveled.

"I don't think he'll like having his picture taken," Skylar warned. "Most officers prefer to stay out of the media."

"I wasn't going to..." Jamie stopped midsentence. "That's him? That's the cop I'll be staying with?"

"Uh-huh. In the flesh."

It was all Jamie could do to mute her spontaneous, *Wow! That is one seriously good-looking guy.*

"Want some good advice?" Skylar asked.

Jamie could tell by the seriousness of the tone that advice was forthcoming, wanted or not, so she said, "Sure."

"That cowboy might look laid-back but he's a great cop. He can be what stands between you and survival. I suggest you don't distract him or let yourself get distracted, either." Skylar paused, then added, "I mean it. Don't go getting anybody killed, especially not my friend, Ben Sawyer."

Jamie had no reply. No rebuttal. The way things had been going awry in her life lately she totally agreed.

TWO

Ben recognized Skylar Morgan from the Denver PD, but the young woman seated beside her looked very different than the picture he'd been sent along with the file on the late congresswoman. That witness had been a redhead with pale skin and large green eyes. This woman was a dark brunette and had masked her eyes with oversize sunglasses.

As soon as the car stopped, Ben put Shadow on a stay with a simple hand signal, left the porch and approached. The car's passenger was fitting an expensive-looking camera into a leather case. He opened her door and stepped back to give her room. "Welcome to the Double S."

She pushed the glasses up and into her hair like a headband, revealing the most gorgeous, glistening eyes he had ever seen. Long, pale lashes were wet, making him suspect she may have been recently weeping. That possibility

touched him more deeply than he had anticipated, although it made sense for her to be
upset, given the scare she'd had earlier.

When she smiled and his heart missed a beat
he chided himself. *This is a job. Get a grip,
Sawyer.* He nodded. "Can I help you carry
that?"

Jamie swung both legs out and prepared to
stand. "Thanks, but no. I'll handle my camera."

As she stood and Ben realized her condition his chin dropped. Tyson had conveniently
failed to mention that this witness was visibly
expecting.

Still smiling, she pushed off and stood. "You
can help with the other stuff, though."

"Right." It was all he could do to keep from
reaching to support her when that was clearly
not necessary. What was it about her being
pregnant that was bringing out his protective
instincts? he wondered. Was that why Tyson
had chosen to send her out of state to keep her
safe? Had he overreacted, too? It was a possibility, although if that was the case it would
be the first incidence Ben had noted in all the
time he'd known the man. And that included
their mutual stint as army rangers.

He met Skylar at the rear of the SUV and
greeted her as he would have a friend. "Good
trip?"

"Fine. No problems. I kept watch to make sure we weren't being tailed." Her head canted toward the front of the vehicle where Jamie was waiting. "She's a quiet one. Kept dozing off. I can understand that, I guess, considering the morning she had back home."

"Where's her husband?"

"Ex. Don't ask. He's so far out of the picture he doesn't count."

"Okay, if you say so."

"It's not me—it's her. She says the guy doesn't even know about the baby."

Ben shrugged it off. "Okay, so what has the FBI decided about the attack at the parking garage?"

"Not much other than the caliber of rifle and type of ammo. It was a typical cartridge. Nothing unusual. You can buy a box just about anywhere for hunting deer or elk."

"Sounds like overkill to me," Ben remarked. They turned together to rejoin Jamie, so he changed the subject. "I take it nobody expects me to play midwife. I may be used to delivering livestock but my medic training in the army didn't prepare me for this particular situation."

Jamie laughed lightly. "Believe me, sir, I have no intention of having this baby in Wyoming."

"Call me Ben," he said with a grin.

"Just don't call you *doctor*?" she quipped.

"You've got that right. Come on. I'll show you to your room and get you settled." Skylar had hesitated, so he looked back at her. "Aren't you coming with us?"

"Not if Ms. London is okay. I have to get back to work. Denver needs me."

"Not even time for a cup of coffee?"

"Thanks, but it's already getting late. I'll stop along the way."

"Suit yourself." He was not about to put his thoughts into words, particularly not in front of his houseguest, but he'd much rather another female was present at all times. Normally, the ranch didn't employ a live-in cook or housekeeper except during the fall roundup. He hoped Mrs. E would agree to stay over, at least for the duration of this assignment.

As Skylar drove away, Jamie lifted a hand and waved, then spoke to Ben. "I want to thank you, too, for taking me in on such short notice and offering to guard me."

Ben gestured at the porch by lifting the suitcase he carried. "I won't be the one guarding you. He will."

His guest stopped so abruptly he had to sidestep to keep from running into her. "Oh no. Not a dog. I don't do dogs."

"What?"

"Dogs. I don't like them, and they feel the same about me."

"That's ridiculous. Why did you agree to come here if you didn't want to be around a dog? I'm a K-9 officer. Shadow's my partner. We do everything together."

"Nobody said a word about that."

Eyeing the patrol car disappearing in a cloud of dust, Ben considered calling it back, then decided against it for the simple reason that he knew his ranch was the very safest place for this witness. Period. She'd just have to get over her fears.

"Then we're even. Nobody told me you were about to have a baby, either."

Pausing and facing Jamie, he noticed that she had lowered the sunglasses to mask her eyes, suspected there might be new tears behind the action and felt slightly guilty. "I'm sorry if I sounded harsh. I can keep Shadow away from you if that's what you want. But I don't want you treating him as if there's something wrong with him, is that clear?"

She stared up at him without comment.

"I mean it. I trust that dog with my life. Literally. He is more loyal than any human and a better judge of character than most, including you. Or me. He lives here with Dad and me. He will have the run of the house but I'll tell him to avoid the loft where I'm putting you. You're more than welcome to come downstairs if you like or shut yourself in your room all the time if that makes you feel better and have your meals sent up. Satisfactory?"

Ben was studying her and thought he could tell when she capitulated. She swallowed hard and licked her lips. "Okay. If it's all right with you, I'd like to go to my room now."

"Fine. Ignore Shadow, and he'll ignore you. Follow me."

Without waiting to see if she was behind him, Ben mounted the stairs and gave his obedient K-9 the hand signal to stay as they passed. He could see disappointment in the dog's expression yet knew Shadow would wait there until he gave a release command.

Increasing wind heralded a change in the weather. He glanced at the cloudy sky. As soon as he got this irrational woman settled, he was going to give Shadow an extra treat for lying out there, exposed to an increasingly cold wind, and being so patient.

Parallels between an impending storm and his own mood didn't escape Ben. It was his sworn duty to protect needy citizens, but that didn't mean he had to enjoy it. It was enough to merely carry out orders. Besides, the last thing he wanted to do was find pleasure in having this problematic woman occupying his private space. He'd never wanted to meld his ranch life with that of his job. The estrangement between his half brother, Christopher, and their father, Drew, had already blurred that line and brought plenty of complications, particularly since he'd stuck his neck out to help Chris land a spot on the same K-9 team in hopes of making amends.

Ben was just thankful his mother, Barbara, hadn't lived long enough to learn about Drew's life-changing mistakes when his illegitimate son's birth had finally come to light. As Barbara and Drew's son, it was hard enough for Ben to wrap his mind around the fact that he actually had an older brother, not to mention one whose attitude shouted their differences like an echo over a vast, bottomless canyon of misunderstanding.

Jamie watched silently as her host placed her suitcase and carry-on atop the bed in the small room. He backed away, seeming almost as uneasy as she was feeling.

"Is there anything else I can get for you?" Ben asked.

"I don't think so. Thanks," she said in the hopes he'd leave her alone before she lost the tenuous control she had over her roiling emotions. Pregnancy did that to women, her ob-gyn had warned, although until very recently Jamie hadn't noticed her moods fluctuating so often.

The handsome cowboy assumed a casual stance, his thumbs hooked in the pockets of his jeans. "Okay. The bath is that way." He gestured with a tilt of his head. "This room and the one through there have been my office, so they're pretty well provisioned. There's a small fridge with juice and bottled water. Check the cabinets for snacks like jerky." A lopsided smile quirked for an instant, then vanished, disappointing her.

"Sorry. I suppose jerky is out," Ben said. "I'll see that our cook, Mrs. E, gets you some fruit and yogurt and stuff like that."

"Thank you. That would be nice," she managed. All the while he'd been speaking she had been trying to not sniffle. "How about WiFi? Do you have it?"

"Yes." This time he did smile. "We may be isolated out here, but we have all the comforts of the big city."

"And none of the drawbacks?"

"Right. Our WiFi isn't password protected, so your devices should have no trouble locating the signal and accessing it. If you get stuck, just holler."

"Will you be staying in the house all the time?"

"No. We have hired hands, but I like to keep busy. My dad, Drew, will probably be inside. He's not well."

Jamie's hands instinctively strayed to her stomach in a protective gesture. "He's not contagious, is he?"

"Of course not." Ben was scowling now.

"I'm sorry. I'm just feeling really..." Her voice broke.

"What?"

Did she detect a tinge of sympathy in his tone? She hoped not because that was the last thing she wanted. Still, he did deserve an honest answer. She cleared her throat. "I guess the word is *lost*. These last couple of months have been really tough and after what happened in Denver this morning, I keep imagining a bull's-eye painted on my back."

Ben was nodding and sidling toward the door. "I get it. I do. I'll leave you to get settled. Supper is late here because we work until dark or longer. There's a clock on the wall above my desk. One of us will check on you around seven and see if you want a meal brought up to you. I already arranged enough for a hungry guest."

"Thanks. Again. I'll try to not cause anyone extra work."

"You will need to tell me when and if you're planning to come downstairs." He'd reached the door and was holding the edge in one hand, preparing to close it behind him. "I'll want warning so Shadow is under full control."

She swallowed hard. Blinked away moisture. Sniffled. "Isn't he always?"

Smiling again, Ben huffed. "Like I said, he lives here. It would be cruel to insist he listen to my commands all the time. Even a dog needs R & R. You should understand that since you're here for basically the same thing."

Jamie shook her head slowly, pensively, and said, "No. I'm here in the hopes you can keep me alive to testify against a murderer and put him away for the rest of his miserable life."

"Protecting you and your baby, you mean."

"Especially my baby." She sniffled, whisked away a stray tear and added, "She's all I've got in the whole world."

The eyes of the formerly stoic man seemed to soften ever so slightly as he gazed at her. He stepped into the hallway, closing the door behind him as he said, "Wrong. You've got me and Shadow, too."

Eating a heavy meal right before bed had never been Jamie's habit and although she had been hungry when the cowboy-cop had delivered a bowl of chicken and dumplings accompanied by a glass of iced tea and homemade cookies, she hadn't finished her portion. Instead, she'd tucked the half-eaten bowl of chicken and thick gravy into the small office fridge and checked her email via the iPad she'd brought. A brief glance at national news had depressed her, so she'd given up and gone to bed. The sun had dropped behind a mountain range by six, she'd eaten after seven and was dozing by eight.

Part of the problem with going to bed so soon after eating was the indigestion the baby caused. There just wasn't as much room in Jamie's abdomen. Consequently, her meal kept talking back to her. By propping herself up on several bed pillows she did finally manage to go to sleep but was haunted by nightmares. One particularly vivid dream about her abusive ex made her fidget and roll to one side. That was enough to stir up her late supper and awaken her to the booming and cracking of a passing thunderstorm.

Laying a hand on her rounded baby bump she sat up in bed. Yuck. The inside of her mouth tasted terrible and she'd learned from experience that unless she settled her stomach with a cup of soothing herbal tea she might spend an entire night of indigestion misery.

After pulling a robe over the loose gown she'd worn to bed she tied the sash, tiptoed to her bedroom door and eased it open a crack. The hallway was deserted. So much for being guarded, she thought, nevertheless glad that Ben's big, black, scary-looking dog was no-where to be seen. If he had been, Jamie would have tried to make herself comfortable sitting in a chair and slept that way. Any sacrifice was better than facing that Doberman.

She tiptoed barefoot to the stairway and started down. Most of the ground floor was visible from the loft and nightlights glowed from strategic areas, augmented by flashes of lightning outside. She was very thankful. If the house had been bathed in total darkness she might have abandoned her search for a cup of tea and remained in seclusion.

The ranch kitchen was spotless, reminding her that the Sawyers did not do their own cook-ing. Of course, not all men were messy. Take Greg, for instance. He was picky about every-thing and impossible to please unless he'd done the cleaning himself.

Jamie clenched her jaw. Was she never going to be rid of those disturbing memories? She padded across the cold kitchen floor, located a cupboard with dozens of ceramic mugs, filled one with water and put it into the microwave to heat while she searched for tea bags. Chamomile would be delightful but if all she could find was plain black tea she'd make that do.

A particularly loud clap of thunder followed immediately by a window-rattling boom made her jump. "Whoa." She drew a shaky breath. "That was a close one."

Tea was in a cardboard box in the cupboard above the microwave and by the time her mug of water was hot she had a tea bag ready to dunk. Yawning, she carried her drink to the kitchen table and sank into a chair while the tea steeped. A sense of thankfulness washed over her as she closed her eyes and sighed. There was something soothing about the quiet of the ranch despite the storm raging outside. Temporary assurance of safety and peace was a special gift, one she would have to thank her host for in the morning.

Jamie spooned up the tea bag and wrapped the string around her spoon to squeeze out the last drops, then laid it aside and carefully lifted the full mug for her first sip.

Lightning flashed in a series that painted a random pattern on the windowpanes over the sink. She paused, waiting for the thunder to follow. As it hit with a reverberating series of booms something cold touched her bare knee.

She jerked, startled, and sloshed boiling tea into her lap. On her feet in an instant, she knocked the chair over backward. It hit the hard floor with a bang like a gunshot, transporting her back to the time of Natasha Clark's murder as if she were standing there, seeing it all over again. That time she'd spilled hot coffee, not tea, and had let out a screech of pain that had alerted the gunman to turn and come after her.

It was all there, fresh in her mind, but passing in a blur of memory and rekindled fear. The stop at the roadside diner. The frigid night. The heart-wrenching scream. The coffee burning her legs. The scent of gunpowder tainting the air. And the blood. All the blood.

Only this time she imagined she saw it bubbling from her own mouth. She screamed. Whirled away. And felt as if her bare feet were glued to the slick kitchen floor.

THREE

Jamie was flailing, reaching for something—anything—to grab. A dog was barking. Hands grabbed her shoulders. He'd caught her! He was going to kill her, too.

She opened her mouth. No sound came out. Someone started shaking her. Gasping, Jamie began her trip back to reality. Where was she? Who had hold of her?

"Easy. It's me, Ben. You're okay. You're okay."

Jamie's knees were so weak she nearly collapsed in his arms. Instead, she leaned a hip against the table while he righted her chair and lowered her gently into it.

"What happened?" Ben was crouching next to her. At her feet lay the dog, head cocked to one side, tongue lolling.

"I—I'm not sure. I felt something under the table and when I jumped I burned myself a little."

"That was probably Shadow. He must have heard you out here."

"I just wanted a cup of tea."

Ben rocked back on his heels and frowned. "Why did you come down here to get it? I told you there were plenty of supplies upstairs."

"I never thought of that," she said sheepishly. "I always go to my kitchen for tea so I did it here, too."

"What scared you so badly? I know you don't like dogs, but Shadow didn't hurt you, did he?"

"No, no." She cast a wary look at the pleased-looking canine. "I was just sitting here, thinking, and when he startled me and I spilled the hot tea, it took me back to the murder scene. It was like seeing it happening all over again." She drew a ragged breath. "I suppose I was primed by my FBI interview yesterday, too."

"Possibly. Have you seen a trauma doctor or is this the first time it's happened?"

"What?"

"A flashback."

"The first time." Jamie raised her hand, palm out, as if taking an oath. "If you don't count nightmares."

He pulled out a second chair and joined her at the table after sending Shadow to guard the door to keep him occupied elsewhere. "All right. I've read the Clark file. Would you like to tell me about finding the congresswoman in your own words?" He paused, studying her. "It might help if you put it into words."

"If you say so." She was anything but convinced. However, since she'd gotten him up and scared him silly she figured it was only fair to do as he asked. "It was the worst day of my life."

With the observant and clinical assessment of a trained police officer, Ben read plenty into her gestures. That same training kept him from asking questions and by the time a few seconds had elapsed he was glad he'd held back.

"You know I'm basically a wildlife photographer, right?" Jamie began.

"It was mentioned." Seeing her peer into her half-empty cup Ben asked, "Can I get you more?"

She shook her head and sipped from the mug. "No, thanks. This is enough."

"Okay. Go ahead."

"I was on my way home from a different kind of assignment. I'd been hired to try to get some candid shots of Congresswoman Clark, so I was in the same area where she'd been speaking that day. As far as I knew, she and her entourage were long gone and my work was done."

Ben folded his hands on the table and waited while Jamie gathered her thoughts and sipped more tea. He wanted to press her for details but figured that might cause her to clam up so he bided his time.

Finally, Jamie sighed and went on. "I'd stopped for coffee to help keep me awake while I drove home. I heard someone scream when I was leaving the diner. Then there was a loud bang."

"The gunshot."

She nodded. "So I was told, later. The noises were coming from the rear of the building so I walked around to take a look."

"It never occurred to you it was dangerous?"

"I'm not a crime photographer, remember? I was thinking that a woman needed help."

"Okay. Go on."

"That's when I saw the man. He was standing over Congresswoman Clark and looking down at her."

"Holding a gun?"

"Yes." Jamie shivered and cupped the warm mug in both hands, making Ben noticed her almost translucent skin once again and wondered what she would look like with her natural red hair instead of the obvious dye job.

He pushed back in his chair for distance. "Okay."

"That's, that's when I spilled the scalding hot

coffee. I guess I must have jumped or something because the lid popped off and it poured down the front of me. I think the pain of that was enough to startle me into moving because the next thing I knew I was screeching at the top of my lungs and running away."

"Did the man come after you?"

She nodded. "I didn't look back but I could hear his footsteps. Knowing he was there helped me run faster, I guess, because I got to my car and drove away without being caught."

"You got a good look at him?"

"Yes. There were lights over the back door of the diner."

"And he saw you, too?"

"I'm afraid so." She was still slowly nodding. "I drove way too fast, I know, but I was sure he was following me."

"You managed to elude him?"

"Hey, don't look so surprised. I knew the area and apparently he didn't because I ducked into an unused switchback on a mountain road, shut off my lights and saw a dark SUV sail right on by. I waited until I was sure he wouldn't backtrack, then retraced my own course. By that time the parking lot of the diner was swarming with cops, so I stopped there. When they found out I was an eyewitness they had me work up a description and arrested a few suspects from a crime syndicate that the congresswoman had targeted. I picked out the guy, William 'Hawk' Hawkins, and the rest is history, as they say."

"That was very brave of you."

Jamie snorted softly. "Brave? Tracking down that scream was one of the dumbest things I've ever done, but the way I saw it, I had no choice."

"You did the right thing."

"Thanks."

To Ben's surprise she started to smile, and he found it encouraging. "It shows you were raised right."

The smile faded as she once again stared into the mug. "If my parents were alive I know they'd be glad to hear you say they did a good job."

"I'm sorry. I lost my mom about eight years ago. I can't imagine what it's like to lose both parents."

"In the same traffic accident," Jamie added. "They didn't even find out they were going to be grandparents. My mom would have been thrilled."

"Not your dad?"

She shrugged. "I don't know. He was always kind of grumpy around little kids." She patted her baby bump. "He'd have grown to love this little one, though. I know he would."

Thoughts of his estranged half brother were

hovering at the edges of Ben's mind as Jamie spoke. Drew was hoping for a second chance to become a father figure to Chris, yet without the older son's cooperation the effort was going to be futile. Caught in the middle, Ben had vowed to do all he could to facilitate a reconciliation but so far he was having no success. Drew was ready but his firstborn son was far too angry about the unfair treatment his own mother, Vi, had gotten at the hands of the Sawyer family to consider forgiveness, let alone a reunion.

"Some men just aren't cut out to be fathers, I guess," Ben said softly, honestly, counting himself among the failures by reason of genetics and association. Thankfully, his mother had been a great positive influence in his early life, but although he loved Drew, the old man was the opposite. He was hard to get close to, even now.

Although Ben had expected Jamie to argue with him because of her obvious love for her deceased dad, he was surprised when she said, "Some men don't even deserve that chance."

Jamie let Ben brew her a fresh mug of tea and escort her up to her room but she balked at letting the dog in. "Uh-uh. No way. I don't want that much protection, thank you."

"I can put him on a down-stay next to your bed and you'll never know he's there."

"No." Her hands were fisted on her hips and she was blocking the doorway.

Ben extended the mug of steaming-hot tea. "Here. Take this and don't spill it or you'll burn yourself worse."

"That only happened because your *D-O-G* scared me silly," she countered, eyeing the beast and wondering if it was half as happy as it looked, sitting there at her feet, tongue lolling, eyes glistening black with a tinge of amber.

She accepted the mug, holding it cautiously. "Tea, yes. Sleep, yes. Dog…no."

"He didn't mean to frighten you, you know. He only showed up in the kitchen because you made noise."

"Oh, so now it's my fault we're standing here in the middle of the night?"

"Well…"

"Look, cowboy, I don't know what you expect from me but remember, this visit to Outer Nowhere wasn't my idea. Being a law-abiding citizen painted a target on me that I would dearly love to shed, but I have no idea how long that will take so I'm stuck. If you want to call Denver and ask that I be placed with some other unsuspecting officer, that's fine with me. Okay?"

Ben held up both hands, palms toward her. "Whoa. Take it easy, lady. I didn't mean to sound critical. Don't forget, I told you you were brave. And I meant it." He gestured toward Shadow who had grown still and watchful due to the change of tone in the human conversation. "This dog isn't your typical house pet, although those are capable of being protective, too. Police K-9s are carefully screened and trained to follow the instructions of their handlers. If my dog was dangerous, he wouldn't have approached you slowly when you were in the kitchen. He would have growled and barked and maybe even nipped you. His constraint isn't natural, it's a result of extraordinary training."

"Ooh-kay." Jamie was easing backward. She put her free hand on the edge of the door as if getting ready to slam it in his face. Ben didn't want their conversation to end until she admitted she'd been too hasty to condemn his K-9 partner.

Ben's quick grab for the door was meant to prevent her from closing it before he'd finished explaining.

Her reaction floored him. She flinched, ducked, squealed as though her fingers were caught in the hinges and sloshed her mug of tea. Those beautiful green eyes were wide and glistening with unshed tears. Her cheeks paled. Her hands trembled. So did her lips.

Ben froze. "Whoa. I was just going to hold the door, but you reacted as if I was about to hit you." His voice gentled, all rancor gone. "What made you think I might?"

Lack of an answer didn't keep Ben from surmising injuries in her past. Serious ones. From a man, probably one she had once trusted, although he couldn't be positive.

He stepped back even farther and hooked his thumbs in the pockets of the jeans he'd pulled on when he'd heard the ruckus in the kitchen. "Look, I know we only met today but you must understand it's safe to be here with me."

Still, she didn't reply. Seeking to make amends, Ben said, "I've arranged for our cook, Mrs. Edgerton, to live here with us, beginning tomorrow night and for as long as you need her. She only went home to feed her pets and pack enough clothes for a couple weeks' stay." Another step backward took him to the railing across the front edge of the loft.

"Thank you," was barely audible but Ben saw Jamie's lips move to form the words.

He displayed his open hands again. "You're welcome. Please don't be scared. I don't know who hurt you in the past, but I promise I never will."

Although she forced a stiff smile and said, "I know," Ben wasn't convinced. The cop in him wanted to know more about her personal situation while his sensible side kept insisting he should forget about it unless she chose to fill him in. Would she be at the Double S long enough for him to gain her confidence? he wondered. Maybe, maybe not. Either way, this vulnerable woman was in need of a friend as well as protection. If he could become that friend and get her to trust him—really trust him— she'd be a lot easier to guard.

"All right, then. Good night," Ben said quietly.

Jamie eased the door closed and he heard the latch click. That should have satisfied him but it didn't. He needed to know more.

Seated at his kitchen table with Shadow lying at his feet, he opened his laptop to research his guest's background. It didn't take long to fit the pieces together and figure out what a bind Jamie was in. Not only was she the sole eyewitness to a brutal murder, she was divorced from a man who had an arrest record for abusing women, which helped explain her negative reaction to his quick move. Given her ex's record and his apparent talent for escaping prosecution, it was little wonder she was so distrustful and so adamant about being on her own.

Parallels between the way Jamie was acting now and the way his half brother's mom had behaved during her pregnancy were painfully clear. Neither expectant mother wanted the baby's father informed. In Drew's case that was apparently because Vi had felt put down by the Sawyer family. And in Jamie's? Ben figured physical abuse had to enter into that equation even if it wasn't the main reason for wanting to distance herself from the man.

Ben shut the laptop and pushed himself away from the table. At his feet, Shadow stirred and looked up at him.

"We ought to turn in, boy," Ben told the K-9. "Too bad you can't talk and convince me to be sensible, huh?"

Tongue hanging out, the Doberman stood and wagged his stubby tail.

"So, what now?" Fellow members of his K-9 unit would understand why he talked to his dog, Ben reasoned, because they did the same thing.

He grinned, his decision made through logical thought. Shadow was nearly ready to resume official duty. It wouldn't hurt to give him a taste of working and kill two birds with one stone.

The moment Ben retrieved the dog's official harness and vest, Shadow comprehended.

He stood patiently while Ben slipped it on him even though his whole body was quivering with excitement.

"That's right, boy," Ben told Shadow. "Time for duty."

Together they mounted the stairs to the loft and this time the K-9 did it sedately, keeping pace with his human partner.

Ben gave the signal to lie down in front of Jamie's closed door and said, "Guard."

This was when he could have, should have, left. Instead, he stood there, picturing the pretty young mother-to-be and remembering how afraid she must have been, both in Denver and during her marriage, not to mention when she'd witnessed a murder and fled from the killer to save herself.

Sighing, Ben descended the stairs but when he got to the bottom he couldn't make himself go back to bed. Instead, he grabbed one of the armless kitchen chairs, carried it up to the loft, placed it next to Jamie's door and settled himself.

Rationale convinced him he was doing it so she wouldn't be startled or afraid of Shadow if she came out again.

Gut-level honesty argued that he was going to sit there all night because there was no way to be certain who her assailant was or whether he had stayed behind in Denver. The way Ben saw the situation, eliminating one of Jamie's enemies was no guarantee that others didn't remain. Nobody was going to hurt this fragile woman. Not on his watch.

FOUR

To Jamie's surprise, she slept soundly for the rest of the night. Drops of rain glistened on the windowpanes like golden glitter as the rising sun began to warm and dry them.

Yawning and padding to the window, Jamie surveyed the scene below. Others were clearly up and working already, and although she couldn't tell who was who, she assumed one of the cowboy types she could see was her host. A flash of memory made her shiver. He'd taken her nighttime foray into his home quite well, considering. Instead of reacting in anger, Ben had treated her kindly and accepted her idiosyncrasies as if they were nothing unusual. Perhaps, in his line of work, they weren't.

And speaking of work… If she'd been at home she'd have opened her files and readied the submissions that were due, so it made sense to do that here. Getting out her laptop and camera she arranged a work area on a table instead of usurping her host's desk, then decided to shower before dressing. The police officer who had delivered her to Wyoming had done the packing for her so Jamie wasn't sure how well prepared she might be. Happily, her suitcases held plenty of comfy, warm clothes, including a loose cable-knit pullover that easily accommodated her baby bump.

She eyed her computer. She felt guilty for not settling down to work, then gave herself permission to seek out food—for the sake of the baby, of course. That made her smile. If that assumption was true, this child was going to be born with an interesting assortment of food preferences.

Easing open the door to the loft suite, she paused, peering back and forth before venturing out. An armless chair stood nearby with a plaid blanket neatly folded on its seat. More importantly, there was no sign of the guard dog.

Empathy filled Jamie. This K-9 cop and his partner had already proved they were on her side. The least she could do was try to make nice with those gleaming white canine teeth and that muscular body that instantly reminded her of being the victim of a childhood dog bite. Truth to tell, she didn't even have a scar to prove she'd been hurt, yet the event seemed so recent it made her tremble inside.

As a thinking, reasoning adult Jamie knew her reaction was absurd. As a guest in this man's home she also knew it was her duty to smooth out the situation as much as was in her power, meaning she was going to have to force herself to let down her guard and try to make friends.

"With the dog," she clarified as she stepped into the empty hallway and headed for the stairs leading to the main floor of the ranch house. Human friends were another matter. Getting divorced had separated her from the couples with whom she and her ex Greg had socialized. The same was true of the neighbors she'd once been able to count on. Relocating and downsizing had been imperative and the less contact she had with former acquaintances, the less chance of running into Greg. In a way, parting from her former husband had been like divorcing her whole life. Staying away from him, however, was the right choice. She had her unborn daughter to think of now. This baby came first.

Her footsteps on the stairs were purposely soft. Aromas of breakfast, particularly coffee and frying bacon, met her halfway down. Her stomach growled and she grinned. "Easy, little one. I'm headed for the kitchen, I promise."

A cheery female voice called, "Good morning."

Jamie kept smiling as she returned the greeting. "Morning. You must be Mrs. E."

"I certainly am." The stalwart-looking middle-aged woman was drying her hands on a dish towel. "Come on in. I've just cooked you a fresh meal."

"You didn't need to bother," Jamie said. Her grin widened. "Of course, I'm delighted."

"Hey, I had a couple of babies myself, ages ago. It's not something you forget, believe me. I was hungry all the time once I got past that first trimester."

"I've been very blessed," Jamie told her. "I was a little queasy at first but never did get sick the way some women do."

"That's wonderful. I trust you're eating right and taking vitamins?"

Jamie had to chuckle. "Yes."

Mrs. Edgerton was flapping her hands as if shooing flies. "Sorry, sorry. No offense meant. I have this habit of mothering everybody. I'm sure you're doing your best for your baby."

"I'm trying." After pausing, she decided to share a bit more. "I don't mind you mothering me. My parents are both gone. It will be nice to have someone like you to talk to."

"Well, you be sure to put me in my place if I get too bossy, honey. The Sawyer men have to from time to time." She gestured at the door as

Ben entered and hung his hat on a peg. "Speaking of which... Sit, sit. I'll get you coffee, too."

Jamie also greeted him, noting his resemblance to characters in Western movies, complete with cowboy boots and a holstered gun. "Good morning. You start early around here, I see."

"Yes. We already got a feed delivery. My dad even went out with me. He needs to keep active."

"Your dad's health isn't the best, I take it."

Ben slid into a chair across from Jamie, mug in hand. "He has his problems."

"Dementia?" Jamie guessed as she stirred cream into her coffee.

"I hope not, but anything is possible if a person gives up on life."

Nodding, Jamie concentrated on her food while she got better control of her unhappy memories. "This is delicious. I doubt I can eat it all but I'll try."

"Whatever you leave will make Shadow happy," Ben said. "He's real fond of eggs."

"Tell me about him," Jamie asked, forking in another bite.

"He's a big pussycat at heart even if he does look formidable. The only rule I have is to leave him alone when he's dressed for work."

"Dressed?"

Chuckling, Ben explained. "His uniform is a working vest and harness. When he has that on he becomes a different animal. It's uncanny. He knows he's on the job and his whole personality changes."

"He's dangerous?"

"Only when I tell him to be," Ben said. "You don't need to worry."

"I told you. Dogs and I aren't compatible."

"Maybe not the average dog but Shadow is different. He doesn't even hang around with our herding dogs. I'm not sure he knows he's the same species."

Jamie coughed into her napkin and sipped coffee to recover. "There are more dogs here?"

"Yes. But they're more interested in the cattle than in people."

"I'll try to remember to not make mooing noises if I'm outside." It was a relief to hear Ben chuckle quietly while Mrs. E. snickered.

The housekeeper added, "You really should get some sun. Vitamin D, you know."

"I do. And I will, eventually. I haven't done much wildlife photography hiding out inside since..." Making eye contact with Ben and failing to get a clear signal, Jamie wasn't sure if she should keep her reason for being in Wyoming to herself, so she stopped explaining.

Mrs. E was quick to respond and pat her

hand. "You don't need to tell me a thing, honey. I know you're in some kind of trouble. It doesn't matter. We're all on your side."

Jamie was touched. "Thanks. Both of you."

"If you want some beautiful scenery all you have to do is look around out here," Ben said. "I'll take you on a tour later if you want. We've got plenty of wild critters. Weasels, owls, coyotes, squirrels, bats…you name it. And, unfortunately, snakes."

"They can be pretty, too, if you look past your fear," Jamie said, sipping at the hot coffee.

"That goes for dogs, too," Mrs. E said, smiling. "And speaking of dogs, that whine sounds like Shadow wants in."

"About time. I'll get him." Ben's cell phone rang as he opened the door. He nodded to the women. "Work calling. I need to take this."

Shadow was living up to his name and shadowing Ben, Jamie noted. Thankfully, the K-9 ignored everything else as they passed from the room.

Mrs. E grinned. "How many dogs do you know who would have walked right by bacon and eggs without paying the slightest attention?"

"I don't know any dogs of any kind, and I don't want to."

"Okay. Your loss." She was crossing the

room. "So where do you carry your gun? Pepper spray? Knife?"

Jamie sobered. "Meaning, if I can't protect myself I need a guard dog."

"Precisely. Stay put. I'll be right back."

Shivers shot up Jamie's spine and tickled the hairs at the nape of her neck. The interior doorway was an open arch leading into the dining room where Ben had set up his temporary office. As Jamie observed her host she began to notice bits and pieces of the conversation he was having with his station. The words *missing* and *presumed dead* made her breakfast churn in her stomach and, despite wanting to give him privacy, curiosity won out.

Jamie listened because she simply had to.

Ben ignored Mrs. E for a few moments, then held up one finger to signal her to wait. This call from Bridges, the special agent in charge at the FBI, took precedence.

"Yes, yes, I'm listening. Another missing woman? Are you sure this Brittany Albradt fits the pattern?" He pulled up a file on his laptop. "I see. Where this time?"

When SAC Bridges told him *Denver* he was surprised. "Wait. The first disappearance was in New Mexico." He looked up the name.

"Emery Rodgers. What makes the FBI think the two crimes are connected?"

The RMK-9 Unit was under contract to the FBI to aid in cases across the Rocky Mountain Region. Ben's boss, Sergeant Wilkes, reported to SAC Bridges.

Bridges wasted no words. "Both were on wilderness trails. Both are in their early to midtwenties, tall, thin, blond, blue-eyed and athletic."

Blond. That reminded Ben of the team's on-going case. Last month, an unconscious woman had been found near a burning car, a baby's car seat and pink baby blanket not too far away—but no baby. The victim hadn't given birth, however. And their investigation had led to dead ends about whether there had been a baby in that car seat. The only decent lead they'd had about the case had been the blond hairs found on the blanket and car seat. One of their handlers, Nelson Rivers, had checked out the woman whose DNA was a match for the strands. Mia Turner had donated the hair for that wig—so they were at square one for suspects. Silver lining: Nelson and Mia were now in love.

"Unless Forensics turns up something else we're considering them separate cases," Bridges said.

Ben paused for a moment, pondering this new information, then noticed his housekeeper waving her hands and pointing to his K-9.

A hand signal released Shadow to go with Mrs. E while Ben switched subjects. "What about my witness here? Any news on that situation?"

"Nothing that you don't already know."

"Thanks, by the way."

"Hey, I figured any assignment was better than cooling your heels off duty."

Ben made sure his back was to the kitchen doorway when he grimaced and lowered his voice. "You might have mentioned her physical condition."

"Why? She can't be far enough along to cause you grief. We'll have her back here prepping for court in a couple of weeks. I'm sure you can cope for that long."

"That's not the point," Ben argued. "What else are you not telling me?"

"It's all in the files. You have clearance. Access them."

"What about backstory? This woman is putting on a good front but I can tell she's been traumatized, and I don't mean just when she was shot at the other day. I mean before, maybe for a long time."

"You'll need a shrink for that kind of deep

dive, buddy. Our job, your job, is keeping her alive and willing to testify."

Lowering his voice, Ben cupped the phone with his free hand. "Did you tell her about the killer's criminal connections? She has a right to know."

"Only if it affects her directly," Bridges argued. "I don't think it does."

"It might," Ben countered. "Permission to tell her?"

"As a last resort," the agent replied. "Your best judgment."

"Copy. So far, so good here, but if something looks wrong I intend to warn Jamie… I mean, Ms. London."

Bridges snorted a wry chuckle. "If I didn't know you so well I'd warn you against getting too close to the subject. One of the reasons I chose you for this protection detail is because you're a confirmed bachelor. Ms. London doesn't look it now, of course, but she's a beautiful redhead when she's not in disguise."

"If you say so." Ben knew it was best to keep his opinions to himself but he couldn't help thinking that Jamie London was plenty beautiful still. It wasn't her hair color or even her rounding figure that defined her one way or the other. It was her kind heart and the love she showed for her unborn baby.

Ending the call he surreptitiously eyed the kitchen doorway. It looked as if Mrs. E had taken it upon herself to try to acquaint their guest with Shadow. That was fine with him. It would simplify the protection detail if the woman could tolerate being closer to the guard dog on a steady basis.

Besides, Ben reasoned, she'd only been here one night and part of the current day. If trouble was on her trail it could still be coming. She could become vulnerable even if she was temporarily safe on his ranch. That was one of the reasons he thought she should be fully informed about the man she was scheduled to testify against. He didn't carry the nickname of Hawk simply because his last name was Hawkins. He'd earned it by being a ruthless predator. And he didn't hunt alone the way a solitary bird of prey would. This hawk was part of a lethal cadre of criminals with connections all the way to the top.

It took a pretty powerful organization to order the murder of a sitting congresswoman.

It was going to take a courageous woman to stand up against such a formidable foe.

FIVE

"Police K-9s are trained to not accept treats from anybody but their handler or partner," Mrs. E told Jamie. "He won't take anything out of your hand unless Ben tells him to." She eyed her boss as he joined them. "Right?"

"Right." Ben nodded.

"Good. I'm fond of my fingers and those teeth are enormous."

"You need to learn to read dogs. Look at Shadow. Really look at him," Ben said. "See the excitement in his eyes? See how his whole rear end is wiggling because he has no tail to wag? And look at his mouth, his face, his tongue. He's almost smiling."

"Um, sure. If you say so."

"I do. Instead of trusting old distorted memories, try making some new ones. This is a happy, eager dog who would do anything, even give up his own life, to save a human."

Jamie arched a brow and leaned back in her

chair as the K-9 inched closer. "You know this how?"

"History and experience. Most dogs are that loyal but they aren't trained to act appropriately, so if they try, they often fail. Police-trained animals are different. They're smarter but they're also more obedient. They have to be so they can be controlled in any situation."

Shadow, apparently knowing that he was the subject of their conversation, had wiggled close enough to lightly rest his chin on Jamie's knee.

She flinched. "Yikes."

Mrs. E laughed and Ben smiled. "Poor baby."

"Me, or him?" Jamie asked.

Ben answered. "Shadow. Look how hard he's trying to win you over. I imagine he knows about your baby, too. He can probably hear the extra heartbeat."

At that point Jamie realized she'd wrapped her arms around her tummy like a shield. Was it possible that the scary-looking dog was actually trying to make friends?

She looked to her host. "What should I do?"

"Breathe, for starters. Then relax. You're so tense that even I can feel it, so Shadow must be really worried."

"Worried? About me?"

"Oh, yes. He lay outside your door all night."

"I saw a chair. You were there, too, weren't you?"

"Actually we were both on guard."

Jamie felt her cheeks beginning to flame. "Did you really think it was necessary to park yourselves outside my door all night?"

"After the tea incident last night, yes. You scared us all when you screamed."

"That is so embarrassing." Jamie hid the lower half of her face behind the coffee mug. "I don't even remember apologizing."

"Don't worry about it."

Unsure what to say or do next, Jamie took the easy way out. "I'm going upstairs to work." She smiled at the housekeeper. "Thanks for breakfast."

When she pushed away from the table and stood, Shadow stepped back to give her room and she kept glancing behind her to make sure he was staying with Ben. Thankfully, he was. She breathed a sigh and felt some of the tension easing out of her shoulders.

Her mind was still on the dog as she reached her room and paused. The door was ajar. "Funny. I thought…" Giving it a push with one hand she peered in before entering, then stepped through. Everything looked normal, yet felt wrong, somehow.

A shiver of warning skittered up her spine.

She started to turn. Every instinct was shouting, *Escape*.

The door began to close, pushed by a gloved hand. *No!*

Reality blurred. A shadow loomed, moving toward her.

Jamie staggered backward, gasping, then screamed at the top of her lungs as the door latch clicked.

"Call nine-one-one," Ben shouted.

Barking, Shadow raced up the stairs ahead of him and was clawing at the closed door by the time he grabbed the knob.

"Settle," Ben commanded, wanting to see a clear target before he released the K-9 to attack. "Settle."

In the second it took for Shadow to respond, he braced himself. "Jamie? You okay?"

One "Help!" was all Ben needed to hear. He shoved open the door and burst in, gun drawn. Jamie lay on the bed, her body curled around her baby bump, hands pressed over her eyes.

Shadow headed straight for the window and shoved his nose behind the drapes while Ben approached Jamie. He touched her ankle. "It's okay. I'm here."

She didn't uncurl but she did peek out from behind her fingers. "Where did he go?"

"Who? What did you see?"

"A—a man."

"Up here? That's impossible."

She pushed herself into a sitting position and pointed. "Oh, yeah? Tell that to your dog."

Ben realized she was right. Shadow had stayed at the window, growling and pawing at the sill, so he joined the eager K-9 and shoved back the curtains. "What is it, boy? Show me."

A feed truck was lumbering down the long drive toward the gate. No other strangers had been around so it stood to reason that, if Jamie actually had seen somebody, he would have come from that truck.

When Ben turned, Jamie was standing. If she hadn't looked so unsteady he'd have left immediately and chased down the departing truck. "Are you okay?"

"Not really." Her gaze kept darting to the window. "Did you see him?"

"Yes and no. A delivery truck is leaving but the driver and his helper were familiar. At least I think so. What did this prowler say to you?"

"Nothing. He just—he just came at me."

"What did he look like? Would you recognize him if you saw him again?"

Her pause wasn't reassuring. Neither was the shake of her head. "He had a mask tied over his face."

"Mask? What kind?"

"A scarf. You know. The kind cowboys wear."

"A neckerchief. I see. What about his eyes?"

Tears filled her emerald gaze and spilled down her cheeks. "I don't know. I'm sorry."

Against his better judgment, Ben slipped an arm around her shoulders. "Okay. I'll take you downstairs and then see if I can pull prints off this window."

"Gloves," she said with a sniffle and a swipe at her tears. "I remember gloves when he reached for me. Leather ones."

"All right. Tell me what you need to work downstairs and we'll take that with us. You'll feel better if you're not alone while I figure out how he got in and out and see that it doesn't happen again." His voice rose. "Shadow. Come."

"There really was a man up here," Jamie insisted. "There was. I didn't imagine it like…"

"Like what?" Ben asked, frowning.

Although her head was bowed and her voice quavered, he had no doubt she said, "Like when I have the awful nightmares."

By the time the sheriff checked in with Ben to report nothing out of the ordinary regarding the suspicious truck, Jamie had calmed down enough to realize how well the K-9 had defended her. That made his gentle approach tolerable and when he again rested his chin on her knee she didn't flinch.

"You can touch him," Ben said. "He's trying to make friends."

"He is pretty special," she replied. "It's almost as though he knows what I need."

"In a way he does."

The fur between Shadow's ears felt silky and very short as she ran her fingertips over it. When he sighed and raised those big brown eyes to look into hers she had to smile. "I may have to rethink my prejudice against dogs."

"That would be best, considering."

It startled her a bit when a big pink tongue licked her wrist. "Ewww."

Ben laughed. "That's how Shadow shows he likes you as much as his favorite chew toy. Get used to it."

Although she made a silly face, she had to admit it was nice to be accepted. "I'll have to work on that."

Still chuckling, he pushed back his chair, closed his own laptop and rose from the table. "Cameras are on and the alarms armed. If you think you'll be okay with just the dog for a little while I'll go see that the rest of my morning chores get done. The house is secure, and Mrs. E will be in the kitchen if you need her."

How could she say no after all he'd done for her? "I guess your furry partner will be enough. When will it be safe for you to take me out and show me around?"

"After lunch, okay?" He gestured at the expansive living room. "There's a sofa in there if you need a nap."

Jamie yawned. "Unfortunately, I am tired. I can't understand why I'm so worn out all the time."

"The shock you had would have spiked your adrenaline," Ben said. "A letdown is normal."

She knew part of her exhaustion was due to the baby, but chose to not argue. It was bad enough feeling less than her usual self without using pregnancy as an excuse for napping.

"You're probably right," Jamie said. "If I go lie down will Shadow stay with me? I don't want him to wander off if I doze."

Hearing Ben say, "Shadow, guard," and feeling the dog perk up and tense was very reassuring. So was the click of his nails on the hardwood floor as she made her way to the overstuffed sofa and arranged the loose pillows for comfort.

As soon as Jamie lay down, Shadow did the same on the floor in front of her. His spine was pressed against the long front edge of the couch, and she could tell he thought he was on duty even out of uniform because he remained alert.

Affection for her new canine friend swelled and she whispered, "Good boy," as she reached to stroke him.

Her reward and confirmation was a fresh lick on the hand. Looking forward to the upcoming photo shoot Ben had promised, she smiled and closed her eyes.

It was afternoon before Ben was free to return to the house, but he wasn't worried until he checked everywhere and didn't find Jamie. He did, however, locate the housekeeper upstairs vacuuming.

"I thought she was with you," Mrs. E said when he asked.

"I left her inside with you."

"I know, but she said you were going to give her the grand tour after lunch. We ate and I went back to work. I figured you'd come for her when I didn't see her downstairs."

"No. Where's Shadow?"

"With Jamie. Has to be. He was sticking closer to her than a tick on a yard dog."

Ben hurried to the nearest window and peered out. His already speeding heart took a jump when he spotted her. Shadow was definitely standing guard, which was good, but

Jamie had climbed a rail fence and was aiming her camera at a small group of wild mustangs his ranch hands had recently rounded up for vaccinating. Those rough-coated mares and their spunky little early foals were cute, sure, but they were anything but tame, not to mention how protective the herd could be if they felt threatened.

Wheeling, he raced back down the stairs and straight-armed the back door, letting the screen slam behind him. If one of the four-wheel-drive ranch carts had been available he would have taken that. Since nothing was parked close by he chose to run. Fists balled, arms pumping, breathing rapid, he ran for the corral where he'd last seen Jamie.

Shadow began to bark. A dark shape whirred overhead. Ben looked up. The object was a drone. Someone was spying on his ranch.

Startled by the dog's bark, Jamie almost lost her balance. Shadow had taken up a defensive position. The dog barked several times then began to growl so loudly Jamie could hear him over the tramping and whinnying sounds the mustangs were making. Mares circled the pen at a trot, forcing the young foals into a small group. Ears laid back, teeth bared at her, the adult horses behaved as if she was responsible for frightening them.

Jamie switched to taking video so she wouldn't miss any shots of the magnificent mustangs. Behind her, Shadow again erupted into thunderous barking, putting so much into it his front feet actually lifted off the ground with the effort. Clearly, he wanted her away from the agitated horses.

Letting the camera hang from its neck strap she leaned to grab the fence with both hands and maintain her balance, then swung one leg over so she had both feet on the outside. That simple movement would have been graceful if she had not had the baby in the way of a controlled descent.

There was a tug on the leg of her jeans near the ankle. Jamie looked down. Shadow had taken hold and was pulling. So much for being friendly.

"No! Let go!"

The K-9 not only ignored her, his angry barking had brought a motley assortment of farm dogs and they were joining the chorus. The din was enough to panic the wild horses and cause them to bunch up against the side of the pen.

The rail fence shook, vibrated, made creaking, cracking noises. Jamie stopped worrying about the dogs, pushed away and jumped to the ground. A stomach cramp temporarily doubled her over and fear for her baby caused her to rue the decision to scale the fence in the first place.

"I'm sorry, little one," Jamie started to say.

Suddenly, Ben was at her side, his arm around her shoulders. "That's it. Stay down," he shouted over the din.

Just then, she heard the same singing whine she'd heard in the FBI parking garage and instantly knew someone was shooting. Ben's grip tightened, keeping her on her feet and ushering her toward the barn.

Shadow stayed close. Mustangs were rearing and fighting each other, falling against the wooden fence rails until something gave with a mighty snap and crash.

Jamie shrieked. Ben pressed them both against the side of the barn while Shadow stood his ground, teeth bared, and the herd passed within mere feet. "Please, Jesus," she prayed aloud, "help us."

A second shot whined. She heard it impact the barn. Felt Ben's strong arms encircle and lift her. In seconds he had carried her into the barn and placed her on a square bale of hay. He knelt at her feet and took her hands. "What were you doing out here?"

"Looking for you." She glanced at her grimy camera. "Oh no. I can't afford to replace it."

"Never mind that. Are you hurt?"

"I—I don't think so." Her tender glance fell on the Doberman who was sitting and staring at her with as much concern as the man. "Thank you. Both of you."

"What started Shadow barking, the drone?"

"What drone? I thought he was upset at the horses." She shook her camera, hoping to remove some of the dirt without scratching the lens. To her surprise, it was still recording.

"Don't worry about the camera right now. Talk to me. Tell me what happened. Did you see the shooter?"

A smile of relief insisted on blossoming despite the trauma and Jamie didn't fight it. "No, but never mind that," she said. "I have video of the whole thing."

"You're kidding." He rocked back on his heels, staring at her state-of-the-art camera.

"Nope. I wanted to catch the horses in motion so I turned on the video and it kept running while I did my trick with the fence."

Ben rolled his eyes. "That was a lot more than a trick, lady. We'd spent weeks rounding up those wild horses and now they're on their way back to the open land."

"Good. They deserve to be free," she said before thinking.

"Now you sound like the activists who try

to stop every roundup, regardless. I agree the horses should be free. We were going to give the foals health checks and vaccinate before we released them."

"Oh." *Oops. Not good*, she thought, penitent.

"Stay right where you are," Ben ordered. "Don't move. I'll be back in a sec."

Jamie watched him stride purposefully to the barn door and speak to several men who had gathered there, warning them to arm themselves and search for a potentially active shooter, first. Later, he said, they'd mount another roundup of the mustangs.

Using the time alone to take a detailed inventory of her physical condition, Jamie was convinced that no harm had been done to her or to her baby in spite of her foolishness. That was a praise, for sure, and she sent it heavenward. "Thank you, Jesus."

Beyond that, however, she was clueless. Was this most recent shooter actually aiming for her? That was beginning to seem likely after she had disturbed the prowler in her room. Nevertheless, just because one rifle shot sounded like another didn't mean the same gunman from the FBI garage had tracked her down.

Ben had mentioned activist groups that didn't approve of rounding up wild horses. Maybe some of them had been behind the shooting. It would have pleased her a lot more if she'd been able to convince herself that was the case but she was not.

These reoccurring incidents were a wake-up call. Anonymous evil seemed to be hot on her trail with no sign of letting up and if she'd stayed in Denver where she was known, it would likely have overtaken her before this.

Us, she corrected. *Overtaken us*. She was the caretaker of a precious new life. Wanting to call out to God on behalf of the baby and herself she found no adequate words.

Silent tears and an open heart did the praying for her.

SIX

A sheriff's deputy had arrived by the time Ben had secured the yard and escorted Jamie back to the house. He left her with Mrs. E while he explained the incident at the barn to the lawman. "She's a murder witness from Denver," Ben said. "I'm only giving her a place to lay low until the trial in Colorado."

"Looks like somebody picked the wrong safe house," the deputy countered. "I'll get these bullets to the FBI in Cheyenne unless you need it to go to Denver."

Ben stuffed his hands in his pockets. "That's fine. They can transmit the results to their Denver headquarters."

"Gotcha." He saluted loosely. "See ya, buddy. Keep your head down, okay?"

"Yeah. I'm working on it."

Jamie was in the dining room when Ben returned. A spotless white cloth was spread over one end of the oval table and she was cleaning her camera there.

Seating himself at the far end of the same table with his laptop, Ben looked at the Jamie over the top of the screen. "Where's your computer?"

"On the floor with my camera bag. Why?"

"I have some files I want you to read before you take any more unauthorized strolls around the ranch."

"Sorry. I really did think you were in the barn and I could just join you so you wouldn't have to come back to the house to get me."

He waited until she'd bent to retrieve the computer before he rolled his eyes. For someone who seemed so polite and complacent she certainly knew how to get under his skin. He'd been edgy ever since she'd arrived and the longer she stayed, the more unsettled he became. That wasn't necessarily a bad thing, he reasoned, as long as it didn't negatively affect carrying out his assignment. If being an army ranger had taught him anything, it was to function well in any situation. That was another plus about being in the RMKU. Several others as well as his boss had the same military background and it helped them still.

Which reminded him of the drone. Somebody had put an eye in the sky to observe his ranch, and he didn't like it one bit. He did, how-ever, hope the operators were activists, riling up the horses to make them run away, rather than criminals hunting the pregnant photogra-pher. It would be far easier to predict probable next moves, for one thing.

Jamie had spread the contents of her cam-era bag on the table with the laptop. Among the lenses and filters was a cell phone. Surely she wasn't still using the one she'd had back in Denver. The FBI had sent her to him via a DPD officer. One of them must have consid-ered the possibility she could be tracked by her original phone.

He reached for it. "This is new, right?"

"New enough." She shrugged. "I got it a cou-ple of months ago when I upgraded."

"The FBI didn't give it to you?"

Frowning, she shook her head. "No. Why?"

"And nobody mentioned turning it off and taking out the battery?"

Her green eyes widened, her face going even more pale than usual. "No. Nobody said a word about it."

"Unbelievable." Ben was already disassem-bling the phone and placing the parts on the white cloth. "Anybody with half a brain and ac-cess to the internet could have looked up how to hack into your signal and track you."

"It can't be as easy as it looks on TV."

"No, it isn't. But for the right person, it's not that difficult, either." He gestured at her laptop. "I'll make you a USB drive of the files on the criminal organization we think is behind what Hawkins did so you can take your time going over it. That man didn't just take a wild notion to murder the congresswoman. We're sure he was hired by some powerful people and you stumbled right into the middle of it."

"The FBI special agent in charge did allude to that but he didn't explain. Just how far-reaching is this gang supposed to be? Could they have traced me here already?"

Ben quickly decided it was better for her to be scared than to be too brave. "They probably have a greater reach than we know. It's hoped that by agreeing to testify against Hawk Hawkins you'll loosen his tongue and convince him to reveal who's running the show at the very top."

"Is that likely?" Jamie had set the camera aside and was opening her computer. She raised her glistening emerald gaze and met Ben's.

It was all he could do to look away. "Likely or not, the smart thing is to be prepared for any eventuality."

"I agree." He saw her wince and press a hand to the small of her back.

"You okay? You did have quite a jolt when you came off that fence."

"I'm fine. Backaches are part of pregnancy, at least so the books tell me."

"It's not a bad sign?"

"Nope." Jamie chuckled. "Simmer down, cowboy. I'm not fixin' to foal."

Ben was not amused. Not even a little.

The files Ben copied for Jamie included newspaper clippings of Congresswoman Clark's campaign as well as her murder. An eyewitness was mentioned but not identified. Offenses which were attributed to Hawkins led some reporters to speculate on his ties to organized crime and seeing everything at once like this made it easy for her to follow that line of thinking.

She finally eased back in her chair and sighed. "Well, that was interesting. Looks like I'm playing in the big leagues when I thought I was on a kiddie softball team."

"Something like that," Ben said flatly.

"How about the video I took of the horses? Did you find anything helpful when you looked at it?"

"I've got it up now. It's mostly scared Mustangs," he said. "I'm trying to isolate some distance shots and enhance them but so far it's all a blur."

"Let me try." His hesitance made her smile. "I do this kind of thing for a living, you know. My work is always high-def. Believe me, if there's anything to see in the background I'll find it."

"Then why give it to me?"

"Because you can point out which sections interest you." She smiled shyly. "I figure this isn't the kind of assignment you usually get. Why did they ask you to hide me in the first place?"

"My dog," Ben said, reaching over to pet Shadow's broad head and ruffle his ears. "He fell and got hurt in a training session so we've been sidelined here at the ranch and I was available."

"Hurt?" She leaned sideways to peer at the enormous K-9. "I had no idea. You should have told me. Is he okay after all that excitement with the horses?"

"Apparently so. I'm not detecting any limp. It was almost time for his final health check before going back on duty. I don't think any harm was done by letting him ramble. I'm just glad he stuck with you when you went outside."

"Yeah, me, too." When she reached out a hand, Shadow shifted position to lay his chin on her knee.

Ben made a joke of it. "Watch it, boy. She'll get mud all over you, and you'll need a bath."

That gave Jamie the perfect opportunity to get to her feet with one of her lenses in hand and excuse herself to go rinse it off.

"Hey, I was just teasing," Ben said quickly.

"But you're right. Hang tight. I'll clean up a little more and be right back to work on that video with you."

He stood as she passed. "After you finish that, how about joining me at the stables? I have some mares and heifers to check on you might enjoy seeing. It's only dogs you're afraid of, right?"

Pausing, she smiled down at the placid, panting K-9. "Turns out I may have been a bit hasty about that. There's at least one I like."

"I'm glad to see the feeling is mutual," Ben said.

If Jamie hadn't been watching she might have missed seeing the subtle hand signal he gave the Doberman. With tongue lolling, stubby tail wagging, Shadow moved to sit at her feet as if awaiting further orders.

She tilted her head and arched an eyebrow. "What did you just tell him to do?"

Ben sobered. "Guard you."

"I thought he was already doing that. Isn't

he supposed to be wearing some kind of police gear when he works?"

"That's usually true, but this case is unusual." Ben was gazing at the dog with a tenderness that touched Jamie's heart. "I think Shadow has decided on his own that you need watching."

"Good boy. Smart boy," she said. "I wish I could give you a treat as a reward."

"The only reward a working K-9 like Shadow needs is praise and a special toy when he's completed a task or a training exercise."

"You mean you weren't joking when you said he liked me as much as his favorite chew toy?"

"In a manner of speaking." Ben gestured toward the kitchen. "Mrs. E won't mind if you use the sink in the laundry room or a downstairs bathroom instead of climbing to the loft." Hesitating, he eyed her as if seeing her for the first time. "The stairs aren't too hard on you, are they?"

"Of course not." A smile quirked at the corners of her mouth. "After all, I climb fences in my spare time." She giggled. "And leap tall buildings in a single bound."

"Not on my watch, I hope."

"Plan B is to keep both feet on the ground until this baby is born," Jamie said.

Hooking his thumbs in the pockets of his

jeans, Ben inclined his head and raised both eyebrows. "And when will that be, if you don't mind my asking. We're pretty isolated out here. The nearest hospital is at least an hour away."

"What if somebody gets hurt?" One arm encircled her baby bump and she shivered at the thought. "If it hadn't been for Shadow—and you and those other dogs, I might have had terrible injuries when the wild horses stampeded."

Did the color drain from Ben's face when she reminded him? Jamie thought it did.

"I've brought in a medical chopper in the past. There's plenty of room to land out here."

"Good to know," she said, forcing herself to smile to lift his mood as well as her own. "But unless I stay here two months, I won't need a hospital."

"You're sure?"

This time she was certain his complexion changed because his cheeks were reddening. "Positive," she said.

"Does the FBI have a contact number just in case they need legal permission for medical treatment? What about your husband?"

"Ex. I haven't seen or heard from Greg since my attorney got him to sign the final divorce papers." She sighed. "And don't look at me like that."

"Like what?"

"Like you don't approve. I don't either, but sometimes there's no other way. Believe me, I wish I had never made the mistake of getting married to start with." Pausing, she patted her tummy. "There's only one good thing about it, my baby. She's my reason for everything."

"Yet you agreed to testify in court against Hawkins."

"Because it's the right thing to do," Jamie insisted. "I may not have known how dangerous he was, but I knew my duty. If I hadn't stumbled on the murder scene, he might have gotten away with it. I can't raise my child to be honorable and brave if I duck my own responsibility." This time her smile was rueful. "I do wish, however, that I hadn't stopped at that diner for a cup of coffee."

SEVEN

Ben knew he and Shadow couldn't resume their regular duties until the K-9 got a clean bill of health so he called headquarters to set up an appointment with the unit's vet, Sydney Jones. To his surprise, his half brother answered the call.

"Rocky Mountain K-9 Unit, Fuller speaking."

"Hey, Chris, it's Ben."

"Ben who?"

"Ha-ha. I haven't been gone that long. Listen, I need to set up a vet exam for Shadow and I thought I'd ask Tyson how soon he thinks I'll be free to come back to work."

"Sooner the better," Chris said. "That new trainer is here to assess the three young dogs we've started working with and I can't say anybody's thrilled."

"Anthony Isaacs has a reputation for being

hardheaded. Has he made any recommendations yet?"

"Nothing very useful," Chris said. "He says Rebel lives up to his name, Shiloh may be too timid and Chase has too much energy. Not a big surprise to any of us."

"Well, Isaacs is infamous for being difficult to work with. Keep your distance," Ben said.

A long pause was followed by Chris's retort. "Thanks, but I don't need your advice, okay? I sometimes wish I hadn't contacted you and Drew at all after my mother died and I found out the truth."

Ben chose the high road and didn't counter with the reminder that the secret had been Vi Fuller's, not the Sawyer family's. He'd tried to make amends by recommending Chris for the K-9 unit but his was clearly not a wound that would heal easily. Ben knew he'd never be able to mend fences if he fell into the trap of arguing about what his half brother saw as abandonment. "Sorry. Just trying to help."

"You want me to have the boss set up Shadow with the vet?"

"As soon as my houseguest leaves," Ben said. "Tyson will know roughly when that will be."

"Okay. I'll give him the message."

Reluctant to let his half sibling go, Ben kept talking. "Hey, listen, you and I should meet up for lunch or something sometime and really talk about things."

"What things?"

"You know what I mean."

"Not interested."

"Oh, come on, Chris. Dad's not a well man. It would do him a lot of good if you'd at least agree to talk to him."

For a few moments Ben thought Chris had hung up. Then, he heard a derisive snort. "After what he did to my mother? No way in…"

Ben interrupted. "Okay. I get it. Just give it some thought, will you? Holding a grudge isn't good for you."

A sound behind him caused Ben to turn as the call ended. His father had come into the room and had apparently overheard enough of the conversation to figure out who he was speaking with.

Drew had hope in his eyes when he asked, "Well?"

Ben merely shook his head. That was all it took for Drew's countenance to fall. Shoulders slumped, eyes lowered, he turned and walked away.

Finding out he had an older brother that nobody in the Sawyer clan knew about had been a shock to Ben but nothing like the surprise it had been to Drew. Mixed emotions had led

Drew to want to at least meet the son he didn't know he had, but the circumstances of the birth and Drew's choice to marry Barbara because she fit his family's ideal image had left Chris Fuller bitter to the core.

Ben felt as if he had been designated as the family peacemaker, he just didn't have a clue how to go about facilitating a reunion, let alone encouraging forgiveness.

He knew how he felt about the tricky situation involving Drew and Chris but it wasn't up to him to preach a new start and win either of them over. His capabilities were sufficient in most areas of life, but he lacked the conviction that he could influence two grown men to forgive and forget. Especially forget.

Ben was certain that his father had truly loved his late mother, Barbara, but now that Chris's birth had come to light it looked as if there had been another love as well. Before Barbara. Before Ben. In that case the relationship hadn't been strong enough to keep Drew from marrying Barbara and it struck Ben how tenuous life was. Lose one ancestor and a whole line would never be born. Leave one love for another and boys who might have been full brothers grew up unaware of each other. That was sad.

Standing very still and pondering his situation, Ben heard faint voices. Mrs. E was apparently assisting Jamie in the spacious kitchen. Good. What little he did know about his assignment had demonstrated how alone the young woman was. She needed friends, especially sensible matrons like Mrs. E who could not only provide advice but back it up with friendship.

Friendship. There had been times in Ben's life, particularly when he was stationed overseas as an army ranger, when he'd had to trust his survival to others whether he called them friends, or not. They had been in it together, a lot like he and Jamie were now, although this relationship was mostly one-sided.

"I don't care," Ben muttered, shaking his head as his thoughts solidified. It was his job to protect and serve, even when he was out of uniform and not working with the rest of the RMKU in Denver or wherever they were sent. The Rocky Mountains provided a vast range of territory and their working dogs traveled to wherever they were needed.

Beginning to smile with satisfaction he followed the sounds of the women's voices into the kitchen. Just because he happened to live where this assignment was didn't mean he wasn't on the job. The main difference with protecting Jamie London was that he was on duty 24/7 with no downtime as long as she was staying at the ranch. Therefore, unless he planned to shirk his chores at the Double S, which he certainly did not, he needed to find a way to incorporate guard duty into his and Shadow's normal days.

Ben let his smile bloom as he entered the kitchen. "How's it going? Are the mud pies ready?"

"For dessert," Jamie quipped.

"Yum." It was good to see the pretty young woman smiling back at him and hear her silly banter because that meant she was probably feeling as fit as she'd claimed.

He leaned a hip against the edge of the granite countertop and started to fold his arms, then noticed something else he thought would carry on the joke. "What's the vegetable of the day?" Ben asked. "Hay?"

Without thinking he reached toward Jamie's silky dyed auburn hair and plucked loose a tiny stem that had apparently gotten stuck when she was in the barn. It was only when she went very quiet and stared at him that he realized he'd made a tactical error. This time, instead of the fear he'd noticed when he'd surprised her at the door to her room, he saw something else. Something almost tender.

Ben stepped away quickly and handed the bit of straw to his cook, pretending he still considered it a vegetable. "Here you go. If you need more I'll be glad to run out to the barn and pick up a bale for you."

"One flake should to it," the older woman said, referring to the way sections split off the ends of rectangular bales and held their slab shape.

"Gotcha." His words were for his cook, but his gaze was locked with Jamie's. Those beautiful, expressive eyes were glistening and her lashes showed a tinge of the red that was her natural hair color. They pulled at him as if he'd been lassoed and made him want to buck and fight for freedom the way wild horses did.

Instead, he managed a forced smile and grabbed his hat and a warm vest off a peg by the back door. "Save me some chicken. I'm not up to tackling a mud pie right now."

Neither of the woman replied. That suited him fine because he had no idea what else to say. He knew what he wanted to do and that was totally wrong, yet he could picture himself wrapping Jamie in a protective embrace and holding her close the way he had when he'd carried her to the barn.

The screen door slammed. Farm dogs met and greeted him with enthusiasm, particularly since Shadow had stayed inside. They weren't bad dogs as a whole, just untrained in comparison to his police K-9. Their natural instincts, however, had stood them in good stead earlier when the horse herd had panicked.

Ben bent slightly and reached out with both hands, petting whichever canine managed to slip beneath his touch. "Yes, good boys. Good girls. You did fine today."

And they had. Recalling Jamie's stumble and how close she had come to injury, Ben paused even longer to reward the herding dogs which were primarily Australian shepherd and blue heeler crosses. What they lacked in formal training they made up for in instinct. Their joining Shadow was the only thing that had been enough to divert the horses and keep the woman from being trampled as well as shot.

Ben straightened, closed his eyes and finally did what he knew he should have done immediately. He thanked God.

"And please help me take better care of her from now on," he added. "She's critical to the upcoming trial."

Before he had time to say *Amen*, he was jolted by the realization that saving Jamie for the trial wasn't his most intense desire. He wanted to protect her for her own sake and for the sake of that baby, too.

And for myself? his confused mind asked. "Of course not," he replied aloud, straightening and making a beeline for the side of the barn. A crew was repairing the damaged corral which had served its purpose when it had given rather than cause serious injury to the animals the way metal might have, but it was a pain to have to replace.

Ben's hat shaded his eyes some and he raised a hand to add more coverage as he peered into the hazy distance, scanning the rising, irregular terrain. There was no telling how far those spooked horses had run. The foals would have slowed them down. As long as they stayed together they shouldn't be too hard to corral again.

Something glinted in the far distance, then was gone. He scowled. Tried to spot it again. All his men were currently working on the fence. Therefore, who or what was out there on his land? Was it the shooter or perhaps the prowler who had been surprised in Jamie's room? Or were they one and the same?

He greeted the workers, then chose one of the four-wheel-drive ATVs that sported a rifle scabbard and got on. "I'm taking this," he called to his foreman. "Keep your ears on. I think I saw a trespasser to the west."

"Want us to come with you, boss?" the wiry man yelled.

Ben shook his head, waved and gunned the

engine. He also had his pistol with him, of course. However, a shotgun or rifle was a lot easier to see from a distance and he wanted to capture the interloper, if he was still around.

The farther he rode the more convinced he was that he hadn't imagined the flash of sunlight off a vehicle. Someone was out there, all right. Someone who didn't belong.

Jamie busied herself at the sink, carefully letting the running water carry away dirt, hopefully without scratching the lens, and looked out the window.

Men crisscrossed the open areas between the large barn and flatter-roofed stable. At first Jamie told herself that she wasn't looking for Ben, then had to admit she was. She'd know him instantly if she saw someone tall, strong, self-possessed and ruggedly handsome with a dark scruff on unshaven cheeks. The cleft in his chin wouldn't be visible from that far away, of course, so her memory would have to provide it.

Several ranch hands were standing next to red ATVs and gesturing as if having an argument. Where was Ben? Moreover, why did she care so much?

She didn't move. Didn't speak. Words weren't adequate when her feelings were running so high. What in the world was the matter with her? This man wasn't volunteering to look after her because he cared; he was merely doing his job. She could have been sent to anybody. Or nobody.

Her heartbeat had started speeding the moment she'd begun picturing him. Slightly dizzy, she leaned her elbows on the lip of the sink for balance.

A gentle touch on her shoulder drew her attention. "You okay?"

With a sigh, Jamie shifted her attention to the kindly older woman and shook her head. "Nope," she said softly. "Not okay in the least. I've really gotten myself into a pickle and I have no idea how to get out of it."

"The trial, you mean?"

Unwilling to explain an unfathomable emotional connection to a man she hardly knew, Jamie merely nodded. "Yes. The trial."

"You're doing the right thing, you know." Mrs. E handed Jamie a towel. "I'm real proud of you, honey. Real proud."

Hearing that was like having her own mother's approval and it touched Jamie deeply. She blinked away tears. "Thank you."

That would have been the end of her urge to weep if the cook hadn't added, "And I ain't the only one who is."

EIGHT

Stopping behind a clump of dry brush, Ben slid the rifle out of its leather scabbard, cocked it to make sure there was a live round in the chamber, then stored it again and proceeded.

Since the recent rains had moistened the ground there was no telltale dust cloud behind the vehicle he spotted ahead so it was harder to decide whether or not it was parked. It was a dark color. That much he could tell. Was there a chance it was the same SUV his FBI supervisor had described when he'd shipped the witness to the Double S? Not likely. Still…

The answer was going to be found by killing his own engine and listening because sound carried so well over the fairly flat terrain, so that's what he did.

The SUV engine was rumbling in the distance. They were either moving or planning to move soon. He didn't care which as long as they ended up in custody.

Ben stood on the footrests of the ATV, raised the rifle over his head with one fist and waved it to signal. "Hey!"

The SUV showed slight movement. He'd stowed the rifle and was easing back into the saddle of the ATV, planning to follow and head them off before they left his property, when a shot rang out. Ben ducked by instinct. More shots followed in rapid succession.

More than one shooter. And he was out there alone.

Smart won over crazy-brave. Ben flattened himself to the ATV, chest tight against the saddle and gas tank, opened the throttle and raced in the opposite direction.

Pistols were far less accurate than rifles so he was glad that only one bang had had the telltale zing of a hunting weapon. That didn't mean he was safe, of course. It merely meant that a hit would likely be accidental.

Adrenaline surged. He felt in complete control until the handlebars were almost jerked from his grip. The ATV wobbled. Swerved. Lost traction in the rough terrain.

Ben fought the steering. A bullet or sharp rock had obviously blown one of his tires. Keeping control was going to be tough but he vowed to escape to fight another day rather than take the chance of firing back at an unidentified source and perhaps wounding innocent parties who were just along for the ride.

Hopefully, his ranch hands had heard the gunfire and were going to join him ASAP. At this point he cared a lot less about mending fences than he did about lethal trespassers.

Angry shouts drifted to him. As his damaged ATV slewed left behind a patch of mesquite he let momentum carry him off the far side, released the throttle and dropped to the ground. Stiff, dead branches snagged on his down vest. He jerked loose, pulled the rifle out of its scabbard again and rested it across the padded seat to steady his aim. He was as ready as he'd ever be.

Sighting through the scope on the rifle he focused on his attackers. Windows were tinted dark, but he could see more than one shadowy figure inside the SUV. In addition, some of the shooting was coming from outside, meaning one or more men were in a position to circle behind him on foot.

"Not good," he muttered, realizing the full import of those words. "Yeah, not good is right."

He started to rise and pivoted when he heard a building roar. His personal ATV posse, composed of his foreman and three other ranch hands, was headed straight for him. It reminded him of seeing reinforcing troops arriving on a battlefield. Clearly, his enemies had seen the tide turn in his favor because those who had been on foot were running back to their SUV.

Ben showed himself and held up a hand to stop his men. "Hold up. We're sitting ducks riding these ATVs. I don't want anybody getting hurt."

"But, boss…"

As they watched, the black SUV backed into a skid, reversed and drove off, bouncing over rocks and through gullies while its passengers fired wildly out the open windows.

Ben ducked and stayed down. So did his men. "They must have four-wheel drive on that monster," Ben's foreman shouted.

He agreed. "And plenty of metal between us and them." He gestured at the group. "Head back while I phone this in."

"Aw, boss" was only one of the comments Ben heard but it was clear all his men were frustrated that he'd called a halt when he did. He sighed. These guys were young and reckless, except for his foreman, and needed to be sat down for a lecture on tactics if nothing else. That, he would do as soon as he'd reported the attack and made sure Jamie and Mrs. E were safe at the house.

For a heart-stopping moment he let himself imagine the worst, then realized he'd been the one in need of protection and the good Lord had sent a ragtag cavalry to the rescue.

And the women? Ben counted, then counted again. Had every man left to come after him? It sure looked that way.

"Who's watching the house?" he shouted at no one in particular. Seeing them all look back and forth at each other, he commandeered the closest running ATV, ordered its rider to tow his disabled one back for repairs and took off at full throttle.

He didn't look back to see if anybody was following. He didn't care. The only thing that mattered at that moment was insuring the continued safety of Jamie London.

Shadow would stand guard over her, of course, but one brave K-9 would be no match for an armed assassin. If he and his men had been tricked into leaving, he was never going to forgive himself. Never.

Jamie had seen the other men in the yard beginning to act nervous. One had grabbed the shoulders of another and actually shook him. She'd turned to the cook. "What's going on?"

"I don't know." The dish towel in her hands was twisted. She leaned over the counter to peer out the window.

Jamie saw an older-looking cowboy step away from the group and start toward the house.

"That's Mr. Drew. He'll know."

Both women and Shadow met him at the door. Jamie didn't like his worried expression. "What's going on?"

Drew Sawyer made his way to the table and sat heavily. His ragged breathing reminded Jamie a little of the frightened mustangs. "Ben thought he saw a flash of something on the south range so he rode out to investigate."

Jamie was out of patience. "Then what? Why was everybody acting funny?"

"After Ben left we thought we heard gunfire. Some of the boys went to make sure he's okay."

"They don't have phones? Why didn't somebody call to ask him before they panicked?"

The older man sat up straighter and pulled out his own cell with a trembling hand. "Right."

Jamie didn't realize she'd started holding her breath until Drew scowled and lowered the phone. "No answer?" she asked.

"Nope. Nothing."

Mrs. E spoke up. "He may not be able to hear it over the sound of his ride. Those things are powerful noisy when they're running. Be right back." She left the room briefly and returned with a shotgun, handling it as calmly as if she did so daily, and proceeded to show Jamie how to load it.

Hesitant, Jamie shook her head. "I'm not ready for that."

"Well, you'd better get ready," Mrs. E told her, "because until the boys get back with Ben, it looks like we're going to have to defend ourselves."

"From what?"

"Whoever shot at you, for starters."

As she pulled a handgun from her apron pocket they heard glass breaking.

Ben zoomed by the barn and skidded to a stop at the back door of the house. He was off the ATV and running before the pack of farm dogs could catch up to him.

He took the steps two at a time and yanked open the screen to plunge into the kitchen. "What's going on?"

Jamie's shaky hands presented the shotgun to him as she indicated the front of the house with her chin. "We just heard a noise. In there."

With a glance toward his father, Ben drew his handgun instead. "Dad, you stay here and look after the women. I'll go check." His concerned gaze met and held Jamie's, willing her to understand what he'd really meant.

"Take the dog," she urged.

Ben's "No. He stays with you" was accompanied by a hand signal to Shadow. The eager dog managed to control himself, but just barely, so Ben reinforced the command. "Guard."

Leaving the kitchen he assumed full police procedure. It seemed odd to be moving through his own house the way an armed team of officers would but the actions were so ingrained they came naturally. One doorway, scan the room, another doorway, then eyeing the loft while checking the high-ceiling living room area downstairs.

Instinct stopped him there. He held his breath to listen. Given what had happened to Jamie yesterday he decided to inspect the loft rooms next.

"This is where I need my partner," Ben murmured, taking each step as quietly as possible. While he was on the stairs he pressed his back to the wall, leaving the rest of his body exposed. That was not an ideal situation but he had no choice.

A thud echoed. Ben froze, aiming toward the living room. Fine hairs at the nape of his neck bristled. A shiver skittered up his spine. He crouched.

There it was! A shot echoed. Muzzle flash from the darker hallway told him where the shooter was hiding. He fired back.

Shouts of "Ben!" coming from the direction of the kitchen turned his blood to ice.

"No! Stay back," he yelled, already thundering down the stairs in pursuit.

Plastering his back to the wall at the opening to the hallway he prepared to swing around and face the assassin. A last quick look toward the kitchen told him his orders were being followed.

He tightened his two-handed grip on his gun, knowing he'd have less than a heartbeat of time to choose whether to shoot or hold his fire. If he hesitated an instant too long he might die.

Duty pushed fear aside. He pivoted and aimed, bracing for whatever happened.

Movement at the far end of the hallway was so brief he couldn't tell exactly what he'd seen but it was enough. Someone was on the run and he now had the advantage because he knew every inch of the house.

Realizing imminent danger, Ben spun and raced in the opposite direction, praying he'd be in time.

Shadow suddenly began to bark ferociously.

Nothing slowed Ben's counterattack. Shouting "It's me!" he burst through the archway into the kitchen and took in the most frightening sight imaginable.

A stranger was aiming a gun at the three

people crowding into a corner while Shadow defended them, barking as if he had the courage of a dozen lions.

"Drop the gun, or I'll send the dog," Ben shouted.

As anticipated, the gunman instinctively lowered his aim and turned full attention on Shadow. That gave Ben only an instant in which to react before it was too late.

He shot twice in quick succession.

The attacker was shoved aside by the power of the impact, spinning away and falling before he had a chance to return fire.

Ben sprinted for the other firearm, kicked it away and checked the downed man for a pulse before turning to Jamie and the others. "It's over."

NINE

Jamie stood back, out of sight, and listened to everything being said as the sheriff and coroner tended to the deceased gunman. Her sensibilities were torn between being thankful the man had been stopped and sorrow for loss of life. Love for her unborn baby tipped the scales in favor of gratefulness that Ben had arrived in the nick of time.

Although the prowler had carried no identification and she'd only seen his eyes when he'd threatened her in her bedroom, she was certain it was the same man. Further proof came when one of the deputies mentioned confusion over just how many workers had originally been on the feed truck Ben had suspected in the first place. If, indeed, this was the same man, that meant he'd hidden himself somewhere nearby and waited for the right moment to strike again.

"I want to learn to shoot," Jamie told Ben as soon as the authorities left.

"Not happening."

"Why not? If I'd been trained when that guy showed up, I could have defended myself better."

"Mrs. E was armed. It didn't help."

"Because he surprised us."

"What would have changed if you'd been fully trained? How do you know you wouldn't have panicked and shot me?"

"Never." She took a settling breath. "Look. I'm not saying I want to be armed all the time. I just need to feel comfortable around guns the way all of you do. Doesn't that make sense?"

He shrugged. "Sadly, it does."

"Well?"

"Talk to me in the morning," Ben said flatly. "In the meantime I'm going to make sure my guys board up all the broken windows and secure the house."

Jamie glanced at the stairs. "It's safe for me to go back to my room? You're sure?"

It wasn't comforting to see his expression change before he said, "Let me have the dog check once more."

"See why I need to learn to shoot?" she asked, meaning to take advantage of his evident concern as she followed him and Shadow up the stairs.

Ben stopped her with an extended arm to

bar her way at the top so Jamie grasped it for added balance. She hadn't meant anything by touching him but quickly realized how comforting it was.

His muscles flexed beneath her fingers. He didn't pull away. When she raised her eyes to meet his she was taken aback by the tenderness she thought she was seeing.

No amount of mental gymnastics would allow her to discount the conclusion that Ben actually cared for her. That moment was so special she refused to ask herself why.

By morning Ben had decided to teach her to handle a gun. He wasn't convinced to let her try with the shotgun but he'd brought it along when he'd escorted her to an open field behind the stables after breakfast.

The sun hadn't had time to warm the air much so she'd worn her coat. Sprigs of prairie grass dotted the mostly bare area and dew on the thin blades dampened her shoes and the lower legs of her jeans.

"You need boots," Ben told her.

"I hadn't planned on making a trip to a ranch. I have hiking boots at home."

Hammering in the distance drew their attention. "What are they doing?" Jamie asked.

"Rebuilding a corral."

"Not my fault," she said with a lopsided smile. "The broken windows, either."

"They'll be on my expense account just the same," Ben replied.

An assembly of gear was piled on the saddle of his ATV. He gestured at it. "Don't touch a thing while I go set up targets."

She raised her hands, palms toward him, as if surrendering. "Hands off. I get it. Anything else?"

"Yes, don't wander off. We checked the ranch again this morning and I have a couple of extra hands patrolling the fences but that's no excuse to relax your guard or get complacent."

"Like I would after what's happened already? I may be brave but I'm not foolish."

He hefted a plastic trash bag and headed for a hill of soil that had been added to the mostly flat terrain. Once he was out there he began to place old soft drink cans in a row on the ground right in front of the rise.

Starting back to Jamie he saw her beginning to scan the sky. "Do you hear something?"

"I thought so but I guess I imagined it."

"You have a right to be jumpy after yesterday." Ben picked up the slim, much smaller rifle he'd brought out. "This is a .22 caliber. Same safety rules apply to all guns. Even a tiny bullet like this can travel up to a mile."

"Really?"

"Really." He levered open the breech. "One shot at a time is all you get to start with."

"The shotgun only holds two. Mrs. E showed me. How many will this hold?"

"For you? One."

When he passed her the rifle, he was careful to point it at the cans and when he assisted her positioning the stock at her shoulder, he didn't let go. His left arm encircled her, and he stepped closer to guide the gun with his right hand.

This was the safest way to demonstrate proper technique but he could tell their closeness was affecting her because her knees were beginning to wobble.

"Don't be afraid," Ben said, ignoring what the teaching position was doing to her emotions, let alone his. "All long guns are held the same way. Get familiar with the proper positioning of the stock so it becomes second nature."

"I should have asked before. Shooting won't hurt my baby, will it?"

"Not a bit. Even the shotgun will be perfectly safe as long as you press it hard against your shoulder."

"Okay."

Despite inner warnings to release her and

step back, Ben held his ground. Was she leaning slightly against his chest? Sure felt like it. Should he caution her to stand on her own two feet or stay put until she'd shot at least once? That decision was tricky only because he liked the sense of having her close and it wasn't until he reminded himself of who he was and what his mission was that he firmed his stance.

"Look down the barrel with your right eye until you see the cans and the front sight at the same time, then line that up with the rear sight."

"Okay."

About to explain about gentle, steady trigger pull so her aim would be true he felt her freeze for an instant. Was she listening? Perhaps hearing something odd in the distance.

He reluctantly let go of her, taking the rifle with him. Shading his eyes with one hand he scanned the overcast sky, pivoting to check behind them. "I hear something now."

She nodded. "Me, too. Where is it coming from?"

"Don't know. You need to get inside." Before Ben had time to give more orders a drone rose over the ridge of the stable roof, its four propellers churning.

Jamie pointed. "Look!"

"I see it." He was in the middle of exchanging the .22 for the .12 gauge shotgun, putting himself slightly off balance. The small radio-controlled craft flew straight for his head, then veered off at the last second.

Ben ducked, hit the ground on his side, rolled and came up in a crouch, out of position to shoot and blinking past the mud on his right cheek. He took a wild swipe at his face with one hand and painted himself with far more mud than before.

"Is it loaded?" Jamie shouted. "Your shotgun. Is it loaded?"

Ben was wiping his face on the long sleeve of his shirt, mostly making his situation worse. "Loaded? No."

"Give it here. Mrs. E taught me how."

Instead of waiting politely she grabbed the heavy gun out of his slippery left hand. Although he could see little, Ben heard her trying to work the breech and thought she was failing until she shouted. "Loaded. Here!"

Ben reached out, groping blindly. He could hear the building noise of the drone. It was coming back. And unless he intended to shoot at it while his sight was impaired and his eyes burning, he was in no position to defend himself, let alone protect her.

Could I do this? Jamie wondered. Should she even try? What were her chances of hitting a moving target the first time she'd ever shot at anything?

She held on to the shotgun. Ben's face was red with mud and one eye had opened only as far as a slit. Echoes of his earlier reassurances came flooding back. *It won't hurt the baby as long as you press it to your shoulder hard.*

The thing was cumbersome and really heavy when she lifted it and tried to keep it in the proper position. How was she supposed to aim? Was there a sight to look at like there was on the .22?

Ben shouted something at her. Jamie ignored him. The drone was rising over the top of the stable roof again. She hesitated, trying to find a way to sight, but everything was happening too fast, too unexpectedly.

The drone dipped again, then passed over them and paused as if a camera was taking pictures. That was her answer! When she didn't have time to use the viewfinder on her camera she sometimes just pointed and clicked, relying on instinct, and it often worked better than expected.

Jamie tightened her grip, jammed the rubber-padded end of the stock against her right shoulder, held her breath and pointed the way she would if the shotgun was an extension of her arm.

Her finger jerked when she squeezed the trigger. Recoil staggered her. A boom vibrated her whole head, from ears to sinuses. It was all she could do to keep from dropping the gun.

She sensed Ben next to her. He grabbed the shotgun and jerked it out of her grasp with a shout. "What do you think you're doing?"

"Saving your bacon." Jamie had almost lost her balance when she'd fired and was so concerned with staying erect it was a few moments before she wondered if she'd hit anything.

By this time, Ben had apparently cleared his vision enough to function because he was heading around the side of the stables on the same path they'd used to get there. She followed as best she could, rounding the blind corner and almost smacking into him.

At his feet lay a disabled, plastic-looking contraption that was actually bigger than she'd imagined when she'd seen it airborne. One prop of the four was missing and there was visible damage to two of the others.

Her jaw gaped. "I hit it? I don't believe it!"

"Neither do I. It's a good thing a modified choke disperses into a decent pattern."

"Huh?"

"You only had to come close because the pellets spread out," he explained. "If shotguns fired a single bullet you wouldn't have had a chance."

Jamie was still shaky but had to grin. "I'm never going to earn an atta-boy from you, am I?"

"Not when you keep pulling bonehead stunts like this." Ben cupped her elbow and urged her toward the house.

"Wait! What about the drone?"

"It may have fingerprints on it. We'll leave it for the sheriff. You're going back inside where you'll stay out of trouble."

"Hey, it's not my fault some lowlife's been piloting a spy camera over your ranch. It's actually a great idea if you think about it. You could use one to spot those herds of wild horses that hide so well."

Instead of commenting, Ben signaled the group of ranch hands approaching and announced, "We took out the drone. Call nine-one-one and see that everybody stays away from the evidence until the sheriff gets here."

The foreman saluted. "Okay, boss. Good shootin'."

Jamie made a face. "Hey."

Ahead of her chance to protest, Ben inclined his head toward her and said, "She did it, not me."

That confession was followed by good-natured

teasing comments and plenty of laughter before she heard one of the men extend the compliment to her. "Good shootin', ma'am."

She was not about to explain the impossible shot so she merely grinned and faked a curtsy as if she were a wearing a skirt.

Ben apparently mistook her action as a weakness. The hand that had been cupping her elbow slipped around the back of her waist and he pulled her to him. "Are you feeling faint?"

Laughing gently she gazed up at his dear, dirty face. A lock of tousled hair lay across his forehead and he was still blinking and squinting. "I'm fine. Truly I am. Target shooting is fun. I'd like to do more of it."

"Maybe tomorrow, after the sheriff has picked up the drone and I've checked in with my boss in Denver on possible prints."

"Even if they ID who's been spying on us we won't know why."

Ben huffed and shook his head. "You may be wearing rose-colored glasses, ma'am, but I'm not. Nothing like this happened around here until you arrived."

"I am sorry, you know."

To her chagrin he released his hold on her and stepped away. "Just part of the job."

Any comfort or camaraderie Jamie had

been feeling vanished like smoke in a gale. Of course, it was his job, his and the K-9's.

Shadow had warmed up to her pretty quickly and so had the ranch housekeeper, so perhaps she'd inadvertently assumed the same was true of Ben. Maybe. Probably.

Upset with herself for attributing affection where there was none, she straightened her sore back, squared her shoulders and marched into the house.

Ben kept going, leaving Jamie to explain to Mrs. E. "I think he's miffed because I shot down the drone that's been bothering us."

"You did? Well, well." Wiping her hands on her apron she added, "Know what you need? A husband to look after you."

"No way. Been there, done that. Never again." Jamie patted her baby bump. "I'll have all I need soon."

She had no reply when the older woman said, "What about what your child needs?"

TEN

While Ben had a private moment he phoned his Denver headquarters to make another report. This time, the regular dispatcher answered and transferred his call directly to Tyson Wilkes.

"Hey, Sarge, how are things there?" Ben asked.

Tyson huffed. "Better than where you are, I understand."

"Have you been in touch with the local sheriff here?"

"Zumwalt? Yes. I talked to him after your troubles yesterday. Why?"

"You're way behind. We got attacked this morning, too. A drone again, just like when the horses stampeded."

"Did it come from the SUV you spotted?"

"There was no sign of it at that time. Makes me wonder if we're dealing with more than one source. Shadow's pretty good at trailing but I still wish I had a regular tracking dog out here to figure out how the prowlers are getting so close."

"Sorry. I can't spare your brother right now."

"Don't even consider him," Ben said. "He'd probably think I'd asked for him and his K-9 just to throw him together with Drew."

"Yeah, there is that. Maybe I shouldn't have let you talk me into adding Chris to our team."

"You did the right thing," Ben assured Tyson. "Chris is a good cop and a good handler. Don't let our personal problems spoil your view of him. Or of me. We'll eventually come to some kind of understanding even if it isn't what our dad would like."

"Agreed. So, what can you tell me about this drone?"

Ben snorted a chuckle. "We'll know more after the sheriff picks it up and has it tested."

"You actually have it?"

"Oh, yeah. That innocent-looking pregnant woman you sent to me is not as helpless as she seems. Believe it or not, she managed to shoot it down without peppering my barns or falling down. She hit it. That's all that matters."

"You're kidding."

"Wish I was. There are so many things that could have gone wrong it's chilling. One lesson on gun handling and she thinks she's Annie Oakley."

Tyson was laughing. That didn't surprise Ben. Every time he pictured Jamie aiming at the sky it made him smile, too. She might be too sure of herself for her own good but she'd come through in a pinch.

"Where were you while she was defending the fort?"

"On the ground with so much mud in my eyes I could hardly see. That's why she took the shot. At least that's her excuse."

"She couldn't have just ducked and let it go?"

"Have you met her, talked to her?"

"Not much. I sat in on the FBI interview here in Denver. She seemed calm and matter-of-fact then." He paused. "I'm wondering if sending her to you was a mistake."

"I sure hope there's no connection between the congresswoman's murder and these latest attacks."

"You realize that it's highly likely there is, don't you?"

"Yeah. Can you believe the FBI sent her up here without disabling her cell phone?"

"What?"

"You heard me. By the time I discovered it somebody could have already tracked her this far. You might want to mention it to the Powers That Be."

"Oh, I'll do more than mention it."

"Good. What's new on our missing baby case? Anything?"

"Yes. As you know, the woman found near the burning car, Kate Montgomery, isn't the child's mother. She's still critical. In a coma. We can't be sure she was driving with a baby, but the evidence leads us to believe she was. And—"

"DNA on that infant seat or the baby blanket will lead somewhere," Ben cut in, thinking of Jamie. How awful it would be to lose a child.

"DNA *was* the key," Tyson explained. "Local police found a car deep in a ravine not far from the car fire. The driver, a, deceased female identified as Nikki Baker, tested as a match to the samples from the baby's car seat. She'd recently given birth to a little girl in Denver so we know we're looking for a really young baby named Chloe Baker."

"What about the father?"

"Listed as unknown," Tyson said. "What is also unknown is why Ms. Baker was wearing a blond wig over her dark hair. Was she trying to disguise herself? Was she in trouble? She died around the same time that the fire ignited in Kate Montgomery's car. How are the two women connected? And where is the baby? Was she kidnapped? So many questions. No answers."

"What a mess." Ben raked his fingers through his hair and felt grit. "Listen, keep me posted if you learn anything more about my witness out here and I'll do the same. I've already posted guards, but it would help if we got prints off the drone."

"I'll mention it to the FBI and see if Bridges wants to assume jurisdiction. It'll be up to him."

"Copy." Ben ended the conversation with a thanks and goodbye, then laid the phone aside. The incident behind the stables kept playing through his mind like a film clip on an endless loop. When he'd blinked away enough dirt to get a foggy picture of Jamie aiming at the sky, his heart had nearly pounded out of his chest.

Then she'd pulled the trigger and stayed on her feet, giving him a sense of pride. When he'd seen that her efforts had succeeded, he'd been so excited he'd wanted to pick her up in his arms and swing her around, feet off the ground.

Between the wet mud, his own feeling of failure and her delicate condition he'd been convinced to do no such thing, but that image continued to return as if he had.

For a person who had apparently faced terrible trials, Jamie London had plenty of spunk left. Matter of fact, anybody would admire someone who had endured a bad marriage yet was looking forward to birth while also agreeing to testify in a murder trial. Any one of those things would have crushed most women. At least he thought so.

Ben's late mother, Barbara, came to mind. If she had even dreamed that Drew, the love of her life, had fathered another son before marrying her, she would probably have had a breakdown. Ben knew it was guilt that was now affecting his father so strongly. He didn't blame him for feeling bad about leaving Vi for Barbara but he did wish Chris hadn't grown up halfway across the country, feeling abandoned because his mother had been ostracized by the entire Sawyer clan.

A lot of different elements had kept Ben, himself, from committing to married life, including family history, since his ancestors had such terrible track records. Add to that his experience as a ranger and you had a firm decision. The army had toughened him up, sure, but it had also shown him how hard life could be and how painful it was to lose loved ones.

He and many of his fellow troops had dealt with seeing so much death by walling off their emotions, including romantic involvement. Especially marriage. It wasn't safe to love like that. Look at what his father was going through, and his mistakes had occurred thirty-plus years ago.

Besides, Ben added to affirm his thoughts, no woman would be happy and content if she was left behind on the ranch while his duty with Shadow took him all over the Rockies. Living single greatly simplified his life and he was more than satisfied to leave it that way.

A shocking urge to return to Jamie, to stay by her side no matter what, washed over him like a flash flood. The feeling made him decidedly uncomfortable. It also reminded him that watching over her was his *job*. There was nothing wrong with wanting to do his best under any circumstances, even ones that left him uneasy and made his gut churn. Too bad she was so pretty and so...

Ben paused to consider the direction his mind was taking him in. Yes, Jamie was pretty, even with her natural red hair dyed dark. But she was so much more than that. She was brave, resilient, intelligent, gifted artistically and the best natural shot he'd ever seen, although he doubted she'd be able to hit a drone the second time because she'd start thinking about it and hesitate just long enough to miss. It happened to the best of instinctive marksmen until they'd had it trained out of them.

She would fit here on the Double S, his thoughts insisted.

Ben shook if off. "No. No way. For one thing, it would be too hard on Dad." *And on me*, he added silently. *I'm set in my ways and happy with the status quo.*

The truth that lingered in the back of his mind was that he was also lonely. It wasn't so bad on the job or when he was training Shadow, but coming home to his father's depressed state and having to deal with the problems on the ranch all by himself was starting to wear on him.

Ben laid a hand on the dog's broad head, gaining comfort. "I'm fine. Just fine." Confiding in his K-9 when he needed to unburden himself was safer than talking to humans. People were too complicated. Too apt to disappoint or not care enough. Or lie. After all, the one man he'd thought most highly of had been fooling his late mother for all of her adult life. In a way, Drew's current suffering had been well-earned.

That conclusion hurt. But it wasn't wrong. Above all, Ben vowed to never hurt anybody by skirting the truth. As long as it was in his power he was going to be totally honest no matter who it hurt. Even if it was himself.

Jamie had finished checking her email and reading Denver news while she waited for Ben to return. A distant thumping cadence made her scowl. Its increasing volume took her to the window, then on to the kitchen to join Mrs. E. "Do you hear that?"

The older woman nodded. "Sounds like a chopper circling."

"That's what I thought. Why would one be all the way out here?"

"I don't know. Ask Ben."

"Ask me what?" His hair was wet, and he was tucking in a plaid Western shirt.

Jamie grabbed on to the edge of the kitchen counter to steady herself to ask. "Is that helicopter we hear dangerous? Should I hide?"

"No." Joining her, he peered at an open field beyond the yard. "Black with no identification is a pretty sure sign it's federal. Probably FBI or DEA."

"Why would they come here?"

Pulling on his boots at the back door, he looked so relaxed Jamie stopped being so fearful, although she knew she'd be happier once any strangers were gone.

"My boss was going to see about turning

your hunting trophy over to the feds. I assume they're here to pick it up before the sheriff gets his hands on it."

"Won't he be mad that it's gone?"

Ben chuckled. "Only because he's a nosey kind of guy. Between him and his deputies and half the residents of Washakie and Johnson Counties, the chances of keeping the evidence uncontaminated are slim. The dead drone will be in better hands with a federal agency."

He squared his Stetson and started out the door.

"What about lunch," Mrs. E called. "It's almost ready."

"Got enough for all of us if I ask the chopper pilot and his passengers to stay and eat?"

"Sure. I was planning on leftovers."

Jamie stood mute as he swung out the door and disappeared from the porch. Everybody seemed to be taking these interruptions and disruptions of their schedules quite well. Everybody but her. Logic insisted that she wasn't to blame for any of it, yet still the guilt haunted her.

She hugged her unborn daughter for comfort and reminded herself why she was there and how important it was to take better care of herself. It wasn't merely the responsibility of bearing a child, it was love. Purpose. Belonging. For the first time in ages she was beginning to occasionally feel content, at peace, part of a tribe that would have her back in a pinch.

Stepping out onto the porch, she raised her face to the sunlight and took a moment to enjoy the warmth before concentrating on the chopper again.

Ben ducked beneath the still-rotating blades that began to droop like week-old flower petals. Jamie didn't realize she'd been holding her breath until he was joined by two men, one in a dark suit and the other wearing one of those white protection outfits favored by forensic technicians.

She knew exactly where they were going because Ben led them straight toward the makeshift shooting range. By the time the visitors emerged and made a beeline for the helicopter, she was shaky from tension and holding on to the railing by the porch stairs.

"I don't think we need to set extra places," she called through the screen. "Looks like they're leaving."

"Just as well," Mrs. E replied. "The sooner they get that contraption back to their lab, the sooner you'll know where it came from."

The blades began to spin faster, centrifugal force lifting them as Ben ran back toward the house. He paused to turn and wave, then came up the steps, grinning. "Mission accomplished."

"When will we know something?" Jamie asked.

"Soon." He reached past her to open and hold the door. "After you, Annie."

"Annie?"

Mrs. E was laughing. "He means Annie Oakley, honey. I think it's a compliment."

"Please take it that way," Ben urged. "Have a seat and let's eat. I'm starving."

Jamie knew she should be hungry, but the events of the morning had left her stomach upset. "Not until you tell me what just happened."

"It went the way I figured it would when I called my boss. The FBI will handle the testing of the drone and coordinate with the DEA if they come up with any prints that match known smugglers. That's how they managed to snag a free ride from Drug Enforcement."

"Why Drug Enforcement?"

Guiding her to the table, Ben pulled out a chair for her and waited until she sat. "Did you miss the reports in the files I gave you about the congresswoman being hard on drug gangs, and her killer, the one you're going to testify against, being a known affiliate?"

"I must have skimmed that part." *Or my*

brain is scrambled by extra hormones, she added to herself. There was no advantage to making excuses when the fault was hers. "I'll reread the stuff you gave me after lunch."

The truth hit her like a punch. She'd only half concentrated on reading the information Ben had provided because she didn't want to think about the crime.

About the blood.

About how close she, herself, had come to being the second victim that terrible day. And since.

ELEVEN

Ben heard a car coming before they had finished eating. "Good thing you're a great cook," he told Mrs. Edgerton. "Maybe if we feed the sheriff he won't go ballistic about losing his chance at the evidence."

Meeting the uniformed, middle-aged man at the door, Ben shook hands and took his hat for him. "Just in time for spaghetti and garlic bread," he said, gesturing. "Pull up a chair. You know Mrs. E. My other guest is not from around here. Honey, this is Sheriff Zumwalt."

A widening of her green eyes and slight parting of her lips were the only signs she'd been surprised at the term of endearment.

"Pleased to meet you, Sheriff."

"Likewise."

Mrs. E set a plate piled high with food in front of the lawman and handed him a fork. *Bless her*, Ben thought, *she can practically read my mind.*

That was all it took to delay any questions and the group had moved on to dessert before Zumwalt got around to asking, "So, where's this suspicious toy you found?"

In an instant Ben was positive he and Tyson had made the right decision by sending for the FBI. He smiled. "About that. There's been a new development. You won't have to mess with the drone at all. It's gone already."

"Good." He began to scowl. "Hold on. Where did it go? You didn't lose it, did you?"

"No, nothing like that. I just happened to mention what had happened and my boss sent in the DEA to take care of it."

"Can't say I like that," the sheriff said gruffly. "You could have saved me a drive all the way out here if you'd called."

"I didn't know they were coming until their chopper landed."

"So that's where it was going? I had a couple reports of a suspicious aircraft circling low over the valley. Nobody managed to get call letters so I figured it was either crooks or some federal operation."

"You were probably almost here," Ben reminded him. "If I'd contacted you then, you'd have missed this great meal."

"True, true." He forked up a mouthful of the

berry pie he'd been served. "Got any vanilla ice cream for this?"

Ben met Jamie's gaze and saw her eyes glistening with unshed tears. Was she relieved by the way he'd handled the situation? He hoped so because things hadn't been going very smoothly since she'd arrived. Not that he was at fault, he mused. There was nothing in his training to cover dealing with sheltering a witness in his home or defending against invisible enemies, although if he went back to being in the army this was almost the same as conducting a covert operation.

That conclusion actually helped. This was war and his ranch was a battleground, whether he liked it or not. Every soldier occupying this makeshift fort needed to stay on full alert or their mutual chances of survival would definitely suffer.

The events of the morning had left Jamie exhausted beyond normal. Rather than go to her room and nap, however, she decided to wrap a light blanket around her shoulders and venture out onto the porch with her laptop. Her only companion was Shadow, and she was pretty sure he wouldn't be giving unwanted advice.

Ben's handling of the rural sheriff had been so masterful she was still astounded. He'd used distraction and conversational banter to manipulate the man into not only forgiving but also apparently forgetting. It wasn't lost on her that that skill also proved how easily Ben could switch between a casual, honest approach and the kind of perfidy she hated when it was directed toward her. That was partially how her ex had fooled her in the first place and how his promises of reconciliation had left her alone and pregnant.

"Right," she murmured, comparing the two men and finding little similarity. Nevertheless, she wasn't going to let herself be fooled again. Not by anybody, man or woman. If her heart and mind couldn't agree she'd trust her brain every time. Period.

Settling on the swing on the front porch, Jamie sighed. This place could feel cozy when she bridled troubling memories, couldn't it?

She pushed her feet against the wooden deck. Slow, even swinging quickly relaxed her. A breeze off the mountains brought chilly air so she pulled the blanket closer, covering her arms. The more she tried to banish thoughts of the events of the past few days, the more they kept swirling through her head. This led to giving thanks that she and her baby had survived.

Jamie sighed. "Here we are, little one. Just you and me," she crooned softly, as if holding her daughter in her arms. "Mama's tired. So tired. But I won't give up. I promise."

A nudge on one side of her stomach was repeated. Jamie began to smile as tears of gratitude filled her eyes and started down her cheeks. "I know you can hear me," she told the unborn baby. "I love you so much. And I'm sorry for the mess I got us into, sweetheart."

Swinging continued. The baby changed position at least three times before she settled down. "That's better," Jamie said. Beneath the blanket she caressed her child as best she could. Oh, how she loved this little, unseen person. At first, being pregnant had come as such a shock she'd been less than thrilled, even antagonistic, but now? Now she could hardly wait for the birth. For the fulfillment of her dream to become a mother, to no longer be all alone.

A whispered prayer for the health of her baby morphed into a sweet, hummed lullaby, so faint that only she and the baby inside her were supposed to hear it.

A click of the latch on the door made her jump and clutch the blanket more tightly.

"Sorry to startle you," Ben said as he joined her. "We wondered where you'd gone."

"I came out here to work but this is unbelievably relaxing."

"Yeah. My mother loved to sit out here. After

she died I used to spend a lot of time here." He paused. "At night you can hear whippoorwills. They nest on the ground and legend has it that once they sing we won't have any more hard freezes."

"It does feel colder here than back in Denver, even if it is May already."

"The Rockies strongly affect weather. It's not impossible to get a light dusting of snow here, even this late in the year." He gestured at the open seat on the swing. "May I?"

"I should go in. I'm getting chilly."

To her surprise, Ben carefully seated himself next to her and slipped his arm around her shoulders over the blanket. Truth to tell, it did help warm her. That part was comforting. Other feelings, not so much.

"Better?" he asked.

"Yes. Thanks."

His boots had taken control of the back and forth motion, giving Jamie's legs a rest. She settled next to him as if they had been friends for ages and often sat that way.

A sigh preceded her question. "Have you heard anything about the drone?

Ben huffed. "It's a little soon, don't you think?"

"I guess. I'm just anxious to know more. I came out here in the first place to reread the files you copied for me, but I haven't gotten around to that yet. Would you care to tell me the short version?"

"If you like."

She thought she felt his hold tighten. Had it? Probably not, she told herself. After all, he was just trying to take care of her as best he could and after the repeated attacks he was undoubtedly getting tired of coming to her rescue.

A tiny smile ticked at the corners of her mouth. That shotgun. *Boom. Ben hadn't exactly done it all, had he?*

With her ear so close to his chest his voice rumbled as he spoke and reminded Jamie of the way she thought her baby must be hearing her.

"It seems likely that you have been traced here and the gang behind Hawkins is targeting you." She was sure she felt him tense this time. "Prints on the drone should prove it, one way or the other, at least basically."

"Then it's a good thing I took the shot, huh?"

From where she sat it was hard to tell whether he snorted derisively or chuckled, so she leaned away to look up at him. "What? You still upset?"

"Me? Naw. Why would I be upset? A total novice who has never shot a gun before, let alone a shotgun, takes matters into her own hands and fires blindly into the sky without any thought of where the stray pellets are going to land."

"I pointed it away from your barns."

"On purpose?" One dark eyebrow arched. "Truth."

"Well, yes, I did think of it."

"Before or after you pulled the trigger?"

"Um, can I refuse to answer on the grounds that it may make you mad?"

"You don't have to say any more. I get it. We were extremely fortunate nobody was hurt, especially you."

"Yeah, I've come to the same conclusion. I guess God is protecting my baby, huh?"

This time Jamie was sure he chuckled. "It would be the answer to plenty of prayers if He is."

"Yours, you mean?" The notion that he might have prayed for her was as comforting as his presence, maybe more so.

"Mine and Mrs. E's and all the prayer warriors at her church, not to mention the believers in law enforcement. Why? Does that surprise you?"

"Yes and no," Jamie said. "I'd never thought about it before but I suppose people who risk their lives all the time have to have faith."

"We all believe in something," Ben said soberly. "The ones who rely on their own strength or a gun or even a K-9 partner can eventually be disappointed. Being a Christian shifts the trust to the Lord."

Although Jamie did nod she also said, "I agree, except I also know that there have been times when I was so scared I didn't know what to believe."

"The toughest times can turn out to be the best. I discovered that in the army, in combat. The worse things got, the more I prayed and the stronger my faith grew."

"Thank you," Jamie said, ruing the telltale catch in her voice. She sniffled. "Mrs. E said she thinks I was sent way out here for a purpose. Maybe it was so I could hear about your faith."

"Maybe." Nodding, Ben eased his arm from around her and got to his feet, then picked up her laptop. Jamie would have preferred a few more moments in which to control her emotions but she took his free hand when he offered it and stood, too. Her fingers tingled in contact with his and she noticed the calluses from hard work that roughened his palm.

Her ex had left figurative calluses on her heart. Would the upcoming labor and delivery she faced be enough to soften them?

Grasping Ben's hand a little more tightly, she kept hold until they reached the kitchen. Even the cook's raised eyebrow and smile were not enough to make Jamie let go until Ben forced the issue by pulling away. Losing contact was surprisingly upsetting, although she wasn't ready to puzzle out why. It was hard enough to tolerate the notion of being away from him without adding to her emotional turbulence by thinking too much. Pregnancy had clearly had a negative effect on her common sense and strong will. No way was she going to let rampaging hormones sway her previous sensible decisions.

Meaning? Jamie asked herself.

Meaning I am in serious trouble if I let myself misinterpret this man's gentleness and care as anything but what he keeps saying it is—a good cop just doing his job.

There was so much truth in that conclusion it brought new tears to her eyes. Upset at herself she swiped them away with a corner of the blanket.

Ben looked quizzical when he laid a hand lightly on her shoulder. "How can I help?"

Jumping back, Jamie almost knocked a chair over the way she had that first night when she'd come down to make tea.

"Don't," she said flatly.

"Don't what?" He looked totally confused.

"Don't be nice to me," she managed through

tears. "Just don't." After one ragged breath she added, "I don't want to like you, okay? I don't need anybody."

A glint of anger seemed to light his dark gaze. "As long as I'm assigned to protect you that's what I intend to do whether you like it or not."

"Fine." She dropped the blanket on the seat of a chair and stalked out of the room.

Ben's "Fine" echoed after her all the way up the stairs and she could still hear it in her mind while she fought to calm down.

A scratching noise drew her to the bedroom door and she eased it open to peek out. It was Shadow, of course. The black Doberman looked so pleased with himself she had to smile.

"Okay, boy, you can come in. But not your partner. Him, I don't get along with."

Tongue lolling, stub of a tail wagging, Shadow wiggled himself through the half open door and turned his dark, expressive eyes to her as if pleading for instructions.

"I could work on my computer a bit if it wasn't downstairs. I don't suppose you'd like to fetch it for me." She laughed and swiped at the last of her tears. "Naw, I didn't think so. Do you play chess? No? Want me to read you a story?"

Feeling ridiculous to be talking to a dog, let

alone offering to entertain one, Jamie shook her head, kicked off her shoes and lay down on top of the quilt on her bed. She had to admit it was easier to tame her wild imagination in the presence of this K-9. He didn't have to say or do anything to impart a sense of peace and safety.

Too bad the human side of the working partnership wasn't this easy to get along with. Her emotions had not gotten away from her when she'd told Ben she didn't want to like him. She'd meant every word. And when he'd snapped back at her it had been a relief because his attitude had helped negate unwelcome thoughts of a future that had begun to include living on a ranch away from crowds of people and the danger they could pose.

Jamie laid her hand on the dog's broad head when he approached. "I'm okay," she told Shadow quietly. "At least I will be when I can be myself and go home where I belong."

In the hidden reaches of her fertile mind was the niggling suspicion that that might never be possible.

TWELVE

The rest of the day crept by for Ben. He'd grabbed a snack in the afternoon so hunger didn't remind him of the time. Rather than go back to the house unless he had to, he chose to putter around the ranch, inventorying feed and animal medical supplies, checking and rechecking the livestock they'd brought in to monitor, even staring at the distant Bighorn Mountains from time to time.

Doing that had proved a mistake because it had let his mind wander and, traitor that it was, it had flashed back to Jamie London. He had no doubt she was capable of caring for a child by herself. She'd more than proved her intelligence and willpower. Ben's problem was the irrational notion that he could—should—continue to look after her in the future.

His faith precluded casual relationships. For him, it was marriage or nothing and that left him hanging. It wasn't easy to think past his prior determination and the promises to himself to remain single. Not that he was over the hill at thirty-two. He'd simply settled into his current life, content to keep the regular routine.

His cell phone vibrated in his pocket. "More trouble?" he muttered, pulling it out and reading the screen. The text was from Mrs. E. All it said was "Supper."

Time was up. He'd have to go back into the house and apologize to his witness. She hadn't deserved an angry retort even if she had spoken first.

It took him an extra minute or two to scrape and brush all the mud from his boots. By the time he entered to wash his hands, his father and the two women were already seated with bowls and platters of hot food on the table in front of them. No one was yet eating.

"Don't wait for me. Dig in."

Ben was standing at the sink, his back to the table, when he heard Jamie's soft voice begin to bless the meal. That was less of a surprise than his dad's clear "Amen" right after hers. How many years had it been since Drew had acknowledged prayer, let alone participated? *Probably not since Mom was alive*, Ben concluded. Whether or not this was a breakthrough remained to be seen but it was certainly a hopeful sign.

Joining everyone else at the table, Ben caught Jamie's eye, expecting more standoffishness. Instead, she reached out.

"Let's start over," she said with a slight smile. "I'm Jamie London, wildlife photographer and crack shot."

Ben's surprise was crowned with a grin. He shook her hand. "Officer Ben Sawyer, Rocky Mountain K-9 Unit and part-time rancher. Pleased to meet you."

"Likewise. I've been told you offered to take me on a tour of the Double S."

"I may have mentioned something like that, yes."

"How about this evening?"

"It's too close to sunset," he ad-libbed, no longer eager to spend enjoyable time with her until he'd sorted out his own feelings.

"How about just the barns, then?" she asked, sounding to him as if the question was totally innocent. He supposed it was.

"We'll see."

She laughed softly. "My folks used to say that when they wanted to string me along."

Helping himself to a slab of roast beef and passing the platter, he kept his gaze diverted while he added potatoes and gravy. "Don't forget I'm still on duty. What we do or don't do will depend on the latest word from my head-quarters or the FBI."

"You haven't heard anything?"

There was a hint of poignancy in her voice so he glanced up. "Sorry. No. The sheriff did report that the license on the SUV I caught trespassing was a fake."

"Bummer."

Ben nodded. "Yeah. I was hoping they were overconfident enough to leave the real one on their vehicle."

He was still staring at her, studying her, when she gave a noticeable shiver and said, "Me, too."

Jamie had been so full and so weary after the big meal she hadn't argued when Ben had delayed their ranch tour. By morning she'd felt so much better she'd slung her camera around her neck by its strap and was anticipating getting some good shots.

"I'm glad we put this off," she told him as they walked into the same large barn where he'd taken her to recover from her encounter with the mustangs. At that time she'd been too shaken to notice much, let alone recall details, so she asked, "What's in here? Cows?"

"Heifers," Ben said. "Cows are experienced

at giving birth. Heifers are the younger mothers. Sometimes they need a little help."

Unsure of whether he was merely explaining or alluding to her, Jamie chose to give him the benefit of the doubt. "I imagine they appreciate it."

His laugh was warm and deep. "Not usually. But if we don't assist, they can die." She saw him quickly sober. "I didn't mean…"

Jamie thought she noticed his cheeks reddening beneath the shadow of stubble that made him look so rugged. She couldn't help smiling. "Not to worry. As I told you, I have plenty of time to get back to Denver."

"Right."

Before she could explain the arrangements she'd already made, Drew jogged into the barn. That was the fastest she'd seen him move multiplied by at least ten. His eyes were wide, his hands trembling, his breathing shallow and rapid.

Ben immediately hurried to him. "What's wrong, Dad? Are you feeling sick?"

The older man shook his head. "No, but you will be. A couple of the boys were out patrolling the fences like you told them to and they found a killing ground."

"How many?"

"Two yearling steers. They're looking around for more."

Jamie didn't have to ask for details. The distress emanating from both men explained enough. She wanted to say how sorry she was for the ranchers and for the poor cattle but chose to just listen.

The more she thought about the situation, the more connections her imagination made. What if Sawyer cattle were being slaughtered to cause an upset that pulled her bodyguard away from her? That tactic had worked before, and a man had died. She blinked away tears and sniffled, assuming no one would notice.

Ben did. He stepped closer to her and slipped an arm around her shoulders. A brief urge to discourage him again passed without Jamie taking any action.

It was all she could do to keep from leaning into him as he spoke orders into his cell phone. "I'll stand down this time, Mac. You take some of the boys and meet up with the ones already on scene so you can give the sheriff's deputies directions to the site."

She assumed his foreman had agreed when Ben nodded and said, "That's right. Now. Leave everything else and go."

Drew seemed to be calming himself pretty

well, which pleased Jamie. His condition fluc-
tuated between being in a haze and acting more
typical. Fortunately, he'd been on the aware
side when action was needed and for that she
was thankful.

Resting beneath the weight of Ben's arm and
feeling a need to pray for the search party, she
whispered, "Father, be with them."

"Amen" rumbled in Ben's chest and sent a
shiver up her spine. Jamie's only problem was
noticing that she had not trembled from fear.
This time, it was being held so close that had
set off the telling reaction.

"Keep your eyes open when you head back
to the house," Ben warned his father.

"Aren't you coming in?"

"Soon. I want to finish up out here. Jamie
will be safe with me."

Drew frowned. "You armed?"

"Always."

The smartest move was to keep up with his
ranch work as he had been while varying his
daily schedule to confuse anyone spying on the
Double S. That wasn't hard when nothing had
been normal about his routine since this witness had arrived. Had it only been a few days?
Most of the time it felt like weeks.

"Do you want to go back to the house with Dad?"

"I'd rather stay with you, if you don't mind."

"That's fine. I like knowing where you are every minute."

"I doubt you meant that to be flattering. I understand. Really I do. It seems like trouble is following me around and catching up to everybody, especially you and your ranch."

"Don't blame yourself." Ben paused and concentrated on her.

"I have to. Every time something bad happens I come up with possible scenarios that lead right back to me. Admit it. You think so, too."

"Given the facts, it's plausible," he said.

"It's more than plausible. It's highly likely."

Seeing her flinch as if in pain and fight to hide the discomfort, he waited, observing. Would there be more? Would she level with him if he asked outright or make him guess how she was feeling?

"Anything you'd like to tell me?" Ben asked, giving her his best professional interrogator stare.

"Um, no. Why?"

"Because you look funny."

"Thanks, heaps," she quipped, apparently trying to distract him.

"You know what I meant. I'm getting used to reading you. Something just happened. What was it, a contraction?"

"No, no."

"Then what?" Considering the color rising in her usually pale cheeks he didn't aim to back down. Not until he got a satisfactory answer.

"Indigestion I guess. I don't know for sure. This is all new to me, you know."

"Pain?"

Jamie nodded and eased down onto a hay bale. "Some. I'm getting to the point where pretty much everything hurts at one time or another. Usually it's my back."

"And this time?"

"A hitch in my side. It's easing."

"I want you to promise to tell me whenever something like that happens."

She folded both arms around her girth as best she could and chuckled. "You do *not* mean that."

"Yes, I do." Judging by the way her eyes were sparkling and she was half smiling at him, he was about to be sorry.

"Well, I did notice a hangnail on my thumb this morning. And I've started getting gas when I drink soda pop."

Ben rolled his eyes at her and shook his head. "Point made. Shadow and I'll check the yard before I take you over to the stable. Can you walk okay?"

"Of course I can. I'm not sure how much jogging is good for me, though. My balance is off."

"Now that's what I meant." Was she hinting for him to hold her hand again? he wondered. Who knew? Certainly not him. Gun drawn, he sidled through the open doorway from the cattle barn and scanned the premises all the way from the house to the distant range while Shadow patrolled farther afield.

Everything looked safe enough. When the dog returned without alerting to anything, Ben gave in to Jamie's suggestion for physical support and reached for her hand. "Let's go."

Thankfully she didn't balk. On the contrary, her fingers grasped his and held tight. They crossed the open area to the stable together with Shadow in the lead.

Brightness of the sun lit the stables via a skylight so it took Ben's eyes very little time to adjust. Holstering the gun, he relaxed his grip expecting Jamie to release his other hand. She didn't.

"You're safe in here," Ben assured her.

"I know. I just…" The comment trailed off as she apparently realized how tightly she'd been hanging on and let go of his hand. "Sorry."

"It's okay. Makes my job easier," he said without thinking.

"I get it—I get it," Jamie said. "I'm just a disagreeable task to you, like cleaning stalls or chasing wild horses."

"I didn't mean anything of the kind." Ben tried a smile to soften his earlier remark, then added, "Actually, rounding up those mustangs is a lot of fun. Not so much that I look forward to doing it *again*, mind you, but pretty enjoyable."

Jamie rolled her eyes and made a face at him, relieving the pressure of his faux pas.

He laughed. "Too much honesty?"

That made her chuckle. "Maybe too soon. I do appreciate being told the truth, though. Are you sure you haven't heard a thing from the FBI? I was positive that their lab would have some results for us by now."

Agreeing, Ben paused to check his phone for messages. "Nope. Nothing yet. But stick close to me and you'll know almost as soon as I do."

"That works for me, especially lately." She eyed the trained K-9. Shadow's tongue was hanging out and he was seated in the middle of the aisle between two banks of stalls. "He seems satisfied, too."

Ben nodded. "Yes. I trust his instincts more

than mine. He has no agenda other than keeping us safe and standing guard."

"Neither do I," Jamie said. "I'm just not as good at it as either of you."

"Wait. Did I hear right? Are you actually admitting you may need our help?"

One corner of her mouth drew up while the rest of her face scowled. "Don't start on an ego trip, cowboy. This is all temporary."

"No argument from me," he quipped back. Expecting their verbal sparring to continue and enjoying every moment, Ben felt his cell phone vibrating in his pocket. He raised a hand. "Hang on. I need to take this."

"Sawyer."

A voice on the other end of the line was familiar. "Hey, boss. What's new in Denver?"

"You sitting down?"

Ben punched a button on the phone and gestured at a nearby hay bale. "We can be. I'm here with Jamie London. Okay if I put you on Speaker?"

"Sure. This pertains to her. We heard back on that drone she shot down."

Expecting her to smile at the reference, Ben saw only a wider glistening emerald gaze. Tension filled the small space between them and he chose to take her elbow. "Just a second, Sarge."

He guided her to an unopened hay bale and sat her down before saying, "Okay. Go ahead."

"There were three sets of identifiable prints on the drone besides others that were too smudged to use."

In the few seconds of silence that followed, Ben seated himself next to Jamie, holding the cell phone between them. "Anybody we know?"

"Yeah. Afraid so. I think it's time we re-thought this witness placement. The gang behind Hawkins has obviously traced Ms. London to your ranch."

"Terrific. Is that all?"

Tyson huffed. "That's not enough for you?"

The pale tint to Jamie's skin spurred Ben to loop an arm lightly over her shoulders and again she didn't pull away.

"Have you made any concrete plans?" Ben asked.

"Not yet. I called you the minute I got this information."

"So, you're not ready to pull her out yet? Good, because I think I've got a fair handle on keeping her safe. Shadow and I are with her all the time and I've got extra men patrolling the fences. We're secure here."

"Except for the drone and assorted assassins, you mean."

"Yeah. Except for those and a few recently slaughtered cattle."

Feeling Jamie tremble beneath his arm he chanced pulling her a little closer and she laid her head against his shoulder. It was hard for Ben to decide if he was surprised or had secretly hoped for that reaction.

One thing he did know. This call had revealed all the details Jamie needed to hear. He thumbed the speaker button to mute and lifted the phone to his ear. "I'll keep in close touch and you do the same, boss. In the meantime, I assume you and the FBI are checking on the whereabouts of the guys who left the prints?" A positive response pleased him.

"Good. Let us know when they're in custody. Gotta go."

Jamie raised her head and swiveled to study him as he ended the call. "They're doing all they can?"

"Of course." Standing, Ben offered his hand again and she took it.

When she let go it was to slide both arms around his waist. Before he could stop himself he was embracing her in return and she was shedding silent tears against his shoulder.

"It'll be okay. I promise," Ben assured her

softly. The trouble was, there was no way he could be certain he was telling her the whole truth this time.

THIRTEEN

A very pregnant ginger-colored mare in the stables had stolen Jamie's heart and made her long for the natural red hues of her own hair. After meeting the sweet-tempered horse she'd felt even worse about bringing trouble to the Double S. Besides the constant angst, they had faced gunmen and lost cattle because of her, too. The longer she remained there, the more likely it was that other living things would suffer, especially the humans who were beginning to mean so much to her.

She still wasn't close to understanding what had possessed her to hug the handsome cop, nor was she sure which of them had let go first. Something told her it had not been her.

While Ben and Shadow did another round of patrolling the premises before everyone turned in for the night, Jamie settled herself on the sofa in the dimly lit living room and opened her laptop. There were no new messages except for a few asking about buying prints from her online gallery. That was a relief. And a blessing since she expected no other income until she completed the crucial assignment that this necessary isolation had interrupted.

Concentrating on her photo files, she might not have heard Ben return if Shadow hadn't suddenly appeared at her feet, tongue lolling, tail wiggling.

"Hi there, boy." She ruffled his silky ears so he inched closer. "Hey, back off, you're drooling on my computer!"

Ben laughed from behind her. "Your fault. You invited him."

"By petting him? Yeah, I'm beginning to see that." She tried to block with one hand, but Shadow was too strong to let that deter him. "Ack! How do I get him to relax?"

One click of Ben's fingers, and the dog sat. "Like that."

"Great. I never could make that noise."

He circled the sofa, pointed to an empty spot at one end and asked, "Do you mind?"

"Hey, it's your furniture."

Although he did sit he also raised a brow at her.

"Sorry." Looking down at the computer in her lap, she purposely let her hair mask her eyes rather than chance seeing that her unnecessarily blunt comment had hurt his feelings.

"I get it," Ben said. "It's been a rough day."

Letting a slight smile lift a corner of her mouth, Jamie peeked out at him past her veil of thick, dark hair. "Ya think?"

To her relief, he smiled back. "Just a tad." He leaned slightly closer. "What are you up to?"

"I started going over the most recent shots I took and ended up opening some old files out of curiosity."

He leaned closer to look, then pointed at the screen. "Where was that taken?"

"At Congresswoman Clark's last rally. Literally her last." Jamie inclined the screen so he could see better. "She'd hired me to take candid shots at a fundraiser she was sponsoring."

"How many pictures are there?"

"Dozens and dozens." Jamie began to slowly page through the file. "I can hardly remember most of these. We had sessions at functions before this, too." A few clicks took her to a previous file. "This is from one of the days when she was acting more like her real self. Her public persona tended to be too formal. I was going to surprise her with these, but I never got the chance."

"Can you zoom in on a couple of faces for me?"

"Sure."

Ben leaned even closer, invading her personal space. His concentration was so high she overlooked the social faux pas. He pointed. "There. Those men right past the drink she's holding up for the toast. One of them looks familiar."

As Jamie began to focus on that particular section of the scene, her eye was drawn to Natasha Clark's hand, to a ruby-and-diamond ring sparkling on her finger. Instead of zooming in on the men who interested Ben she enlarged the section with the ring. Her jaw gaped.

"Not there," he said, pointing again. "Behind her." When Jamie failed to respond he swiveled to scowl at her. "What's wrong?"

"Everything," she said with a sniffle.

"Care to share?"

"I hardly know how to begin. My ex-husband, Greg, gave me a special ring that he insisted he'd had designed and had made just for me." Knowing her voice was about to break she took a deep, calming breath and loosed her anger to help her cope. " I don't know why I didn't notice before."

"Notice what?"

Jamie felt his right shoulder crowd her left one and gave ground. "Look. Natasha Clark is wearing my ring."

"Could you be mistaken?"

"No. That's my ring all right. On her finger. I was so proud of it I looked at it a lot. That one is exactly the same."

"Maybe she told him she admired yours, and he arranged for her to have another made."

"How? He told me he barely knew Natasha when she hired me to photograph her. This picture was taken only a few weeks before her murder. They must have been close."

"Okay, calm down. Let's think this through. Be logical."

"There's nothing logical about it. The way I see it, either Greg gave her my ring after I caught him cheating and threw it at him, or he thought so little of his gift he had a copy made to impress another woman."

"What brought you to get a divorce? If you don't mind my asking. You never said."

Sighing deeply, Jamie shook her head. "Greg had been in the shower one evening so I'd answered his phone for him. A woman's voice said, *Hey, baby* then hung up when I asked her name. That wasn't the first time I'd suspected he was playing around but it never dawned on me that the congresswoman might be one of the other women in his life. No wonder he tried to talk me out of taking the job her election committee offered."

When Ben pushed away and got to his feet

Jamie was acutely aware of the loss. She chalked the sensation up to both her pregnancy and shock from spotting the ruby ring. It was hers. It had to be. Besides, Natasha was wearing it on her pinkie finger, proving the sizing was too small.

Thankful that her marriage was over, Jamie reasoned that any twinges of betrayal she was feeling were minor compared to escaping from Greg's mental and physical abuse. Besides, she hadn't only saved herself, she'd rescued her unborn baby

"Your ex must have been a real piece of work."

"He was smooth. I was totally fooled. I didn't see into his heart, into his core, until it was too late. We were already married. I promised myself I'd stick it out because I believe in the sanctity of marriage, but Greg eventually made it impossible."

"I'm relieved you're not considering reconciliation. Some women give in and go back even when they know better"

Jamie shook her head emphatically. "Not me. Not with a child to think of. Greg would ruin my daughter's chances for a normal life before she even learned to walk and talk."

"Suppose a baby wasn't in the picture."

She lifted her face toward him, eyes glis-

tening. "It wouldn't make a bit of difference."
Jamie sniffled. "I know I'm supposed to be forgiving but it's really hard. What I feel is more
a sense of joy that I was pushed out and therefore escaped. Now that I'm single I intend to
stay that way and do the job God has given me
to the best of my ability."

"Raise your daughter."

"Yes." She was about to close the laptop when
she saw a flash. Heard a boom that echoed.

Ben dove for her, pushing her down on the
sofa. Her computer landed on the floor.

Glass shattered. Shadow began to bark. Mrs.
E rushed out of the kitchen. Drew appeared
from the hallway.

"Everybody down!" Ben shouted. "Stay
away from the windows."

Long seconds passed with no more shots, no
conversation to break the silence.

"Can't breathe. Heavy," Jamie finally said.

"Sorry. You okay?"

"Yes."

Levering himself off her, Ben had placed his
body between hers and the shattered window.
It was hard for her to feel grateful when someone else was putting himself in jeopardy and
she said so. "You get down, too."

"As soon as I check for the source of the
shots."

She made a grab for his arm and felt the taut muscles beneath his shirt. "Don't leave me."

"I'm not going far." He whipped out his phone and notified the sheriff, followed by a call to his foreman.

Shadow had taken up a position of guard, his broad back to Jamie and Ben, his concentration on the broken window. He didn't bark; he just watched.

Ben ended the second call. "They didn't see any trespassers, but nobody heard a car leaving, either."

"I can get up?" She shifted a throw pillow under her head and used her elbows to try to rise.

"Not yet," Ben said, on the move. "Stay down until I tell you. Dad, you go check the locks."

"Where are you going?" Jamie fought unshed tears.

"Outside to have a look around."

"No. Please don't," Jamie pled. "I thought I'd be safe enough in here if I kept the lights low."

"I suspect your face was lit by the computer screen," Ben told her. "A perfect target."

"But they missed."

He caught his breath. "Yeah. Thank God, for real. Are you sure you're okay?"

Was she? A quick personal inventory affirmed wellness. "Yes, I think so." One hand rested on her chest at the base of her throat where she felt a pounding pulse. "Anybody in their right mind would be scared."

"Right. One more call before I go." Ben was speaking quietly but Jamie was able to over-hear enough to tell he was talking to his boss.

"That's right. Somebody put a bullet right through my living room window. No, I'm not kidding. That's it. She can't stay here any longer. It's not safe enough."

After a short pause, Ben said, "No. We can't wait. I have to get her out of here ASAP." He began to pace.

Jamie was concentrating so hard on what he was saying she failed to notice where he stepped until his boots crunched on broken glass. Apparently, Ben hadn't been aware of his path either because he started to withdraw.

Another shot echoed. This time the bullet punched a neat little hole through the drapery and impacted the back of the couch. Where she'd been sitting. Where Ben had been sitting.

He drew his pistol, diving for the floor and coming up right next to the damaged window. One hand held his gun ready. The other eased back a tiny corner of the drape so he could peek out.

Jamie couldn't decide whether she hoped he'd report seeing nothing or the opposite. Either would be terrifying in its own way. His shoulder muscles flexed beneath his shirt.

She was about to ask him if he saw anybody when he shifted his pistol, took aim and froze. As soon as another incoming bullet hit the window he began returning fire.

Jamie gritted her teeth and covered her ears. *How much worse could things get?*

A lot worse, she answered as she felt her low backache spreading around her sides and contracting her stomach muscles. Her mind screamed, *No!* She breathed rapidly. Her heart was pounding. And then the sensation eased.

She was about to relax and send up a prayer of thanks when it happened again. By the third time she'd decided she was in serious trouble.

FOURTEEN

Shooting stopped. Silence lay heavy. Ben's nerves were on edge while his thoughts scattered. If he left the house to patrol the yard with his men he'd be leaving only Shadow to guard Jamie. If he didn't go in pursuit until local police arrived, he'd have to call on his ranch hands for backup and expose them to danger because they were untrained in police work. It was a no-win situation.

His cell phone rang. "Sawyer."

"It's me, boss," the foreman said. "We can't figure where that last shot came from. You were shooting back. Did you see something?"

"A flash and the shadow of a running man. Behind the east corner of the stables. I knew it was too far for accuracy but I wanted whoever it was to know we weren't sitting ducks."

"Gotcha. A couple of us will head over that way now and check it out. Hold your fire, okay?"

"Gladly." He reloaded his gun before sticking it back into the holster at his waist.

Jamie had gone into the kitchen with Mrs. E and he didn't think anything of it until he followed them. His very pregnant witness was sitting at the kitchen table. Her face was pale yet her cheeks were red. Too red.

Pulling up a chair next to her, Ben took her hand. "What's wrong?"

She merely shook her head so he looked to his cook-housekeeper. "Mrs. E?"

"Likely it was those Braxton-Hicks contractions. They can be scary when you've never felt the real thing. Believe me, they may squeeze a tad, but they're not serious."

Ben leaned closer. "You had contractions? Was it my fault?"

"What?" Her brow knit, her eyes narrowing. "Why would it be your fault?"

"I pushed you over on the couch."

"To save my life. Feel free to do that anytime I'm being shot at, okay?" She pulled a face. "Believe me, that had nothing to do with it. I didn't start feeling funny until just a minute ago." One hand rested on her abdomen, the other elbow was propped on the table. "Nothing's going on now. Maybe the baby just stretched too far and pinched a nerve or something."

Already researching kinds of contractions on his phone, Ben was relieved to see that first-time mothers were often confused by twinges of pain or mild, preliminary contractions that never progressed into labor.

"Okay. When you feel up to it I want you to go upstairs and pack for travel."

"You got word of a new safe house?"

"No. But I have thought of another place we can go to until somebody above my pay grade finally acts." Hesitating, he studied her. "You'd tell me if you were in real labor, right?"

"Of course. Why?"

"Because the hideaway I have in mind is a cabin in the wilderness, very isolated, and I won't take you there if there's any chance you're getting ready to give birth."

"Can't be. Too soon by at least five weeks. Besides, Mrs. E says I'm fine, and we don't want to argue with the voice of experience."

"Okay. Get some rest. We won't leave right away. Travelling at night would mean we'd be less likely to be spotted but it would also keep us from seeing enemies. I want you to go pack, like I said, then try to get some sleep. Shadow will be right outside your door and I'll station a couple of my men to guard your window."

"Can I let Shadow in if I want?" Jamie asked sheepishly.

"Even better. I may actually be able to get a decent night's sleep when I know he's right at your feet."

Ben grabbed his hat and vest, then a flashlight. "I'm still going to help the boys search the yard, make sure they didn't miss anything." Concerned, he faced Jamie. "One more twinge and the trip is off, understand? You'll tell me the truth? Promise?"

"I promise," Jamie said with a smile. "Did anybody ever tell you that you worry too much?"

The banging screen door almost covered his blunt "No."

Once Jamie had answered a few personal biological questions, the cook seemed satisfied. "You're fine," she said. "Trust me. I've had a passel of kids. No two labors were alike, but they were all unmistakable. I had no doubt what was happening."

"In other words, it hurts."

The cook smiled gently and patted Jamie's hand. "Not so much that it stops most women from having more babies. Besides, you can always ask for drugs to ease it."

"I don't want to hurt my baby."

"If you need medicine to help you, there's nothing wrong with taking it. After all, the

Good Lord made the plants that they use to make drugs."

"How are you feeling now? Any more contractions?"

"Nope. Not a twinge," Jamie said. "Thanks for calming me down."

"I think you should leave your door ajar tonight. That way, if you do have trouble we'll be able to hear you call out."

"Okay. But I won't have any trouble. I know I won't. I really do feel great. Tired, of course, but wonderful." She got to her feet with a sigh, leaning on the edge of the heavy table for support. "I'm going to go up and pack, then crash, if you don't mind."

"Do you need my help?"

Jamie smiled gently at the K-9 who had risen to stand at her side and gaze up at her with big brown eyes. "All I'll need is my friend Shadow. He and I are joined at the hip now."

"Couldn't ask for a better companion," Mrs. E said.

Although Jamie nodded, she was picturing a stalwart cowboy cop standing with her and the dog. A man whose life she had turned upside down and damaged just by being herself. If she ever did weaken and decide to consider marrying again, she'd be hard put to find anyone as brave and appealing and considerate yet strong and honest as Ben Sawyer.

She huffed to herself as she climbed the stairs to the loft. The perfect man didn't exist. Everybody knew that. No one was ideal. Beyond good looks there were so many traits to consider that it boggled the mind. Plus, there was the ability many people had to carry off a pretense so seamlessly that they could fool everyone, especially a smitten and naive woman like she had once been. Greg had done that to her. She had never wanted to believe he could be so unfaithful and cruel until she'd run out of excuses to deny the truth.

"Here we are, Shadow," she said, gesturing a welcome. "Come on in. You can watch me pack."

The joy in the Doberman's countenance was evident. His step was light and athletic, his eyes twinkled and when he turned to look up at her she almost thought he was smiling.

"Too bad I haven't been able to get over my distrust of people the way I got over being afraid of you," Jamie told him.

Hearing those words spoken and taking them in, she was struck by the notion that her determination to stay single might actually be fueled by fear instead of merely determination. That was a new concept. One she didn't like a bit.

Fear? Surely not. Just because she happened to have decided it was smarter to remain un-married was no reason to suspect she was actu-ally frightened. She'd faced bobcats and eagles, venomous snakes and more in the wild, taking photographs that were winning awards. There could be no doubt she had courage. Plenty of it.

She plopped down on the edge of the bed and Shadow immediately rested his chin on her knee. The baby began to kick, a reminder of her current priorities. She touched the inside of the third finger of her left hand with her thumb just as she had when she's still worn the precious ruby-and-diamond ring. Seeing her former trea-sure on Natasha's finger had hurt. A lot.

"It wasn't just a ring," Jamie told the dog. "It was the promises it represented. I so wanted to believe Greg was going to change and we could save our marriage. What a fool I was."

The Doberman scooted closer, clearly show-ing empathy. Jamie would have leaned down to hug him in spite of the rules against it if her baby bump hadn't been in the way. Instead, she stood and made her way to the window. Some-one had thoughtfully drawn the heavy drapes.

She turned off interior lights before chanc-ing a peek outside. Floodlights bathed the yard below. Men were moving around in groups of two or three and an occasional beam told her they were carrying flashlights, too.

This time she knew exactly which one was Ben. *How?* She had no idea, she simply let her gaze travel over the men until it stopped at one particular figure. Not only was she positive she was looking at him, she felt a jolt of excitement. Of joy.

Her hand was at her throat. Her pulse was faster than normal. And, wonder of wonders, she couldn't think of a single reason to reject him. That was very troubling.

Jamie made a face as she let go of the drape. *No. No, no, no.* She refused to consider the notion that God had sent her all the way to Wyoming for any reason other than protection from assassins. Wasn't that enough? Sure seemed like plenty to her. At least it had until she'd arrived at the Double S.

"If only I hadn't seen that murder," she murmured. Her life was filled with *if only*'s, especially the last few years, such as marriage to a man who seemed to derive pleasure from fooling people, from hurting her. If only he hadn't cheated and insisted he was faithful. If only his cruelty and lies hadn't led to divorce. And if only she hadn't accepted the job of taking promo pics for the congresswoman despite Greg's objections.

No wonder he hadn't wanted her underfoot when Natasha was campaigning. The presence of a wife cramped his style.

Lifting misty eyes toward the stars in heaven, Jamie spoke to God. "I'm sorry I didn't listen to You, Father. I know those uneasy feelings were a warning and I let Greg sweep me off my feet anyway." Tears began to slide down her cheeks. "I'm so sorry. Please forgive me and protect my baby. None of this is her fault."

A sense of peace enveloped her as if someone had just wrapped her in a warm blanket. She hugged her unborn child to share the comfort and whispered more prayers of thanks.

The baby kicked against her open hand. Jamie sniffled. Then she smiled. "I get it. I do. And I am thankful for everything in spite of my past mistakes."

Had she finally taken the steps necessary to reach a stage of personal forgiveness that included her ex? Parts of her brain denied it. More tender parts of her psyche thought she might actually have turned a corner.

Although the overall sense of peace remained with her, she was nonetheless unsure. The more she pondered her turbulent feelings, the more confused she grew. "I don't want to forgive Greg," she admitted ruefully.

Could that be true? Was her latent anger

keeping her from moving forward into the future on faith?

Weariness suddenly overwhelmed her. She made her way to the bed, Shadow at her side, and lay down. "Just a few minutes," she told the dog tenderly. "Just let me rest a bit and I'll start packing."

It didn't seem at all odd to be unburdening herself to the intelligent K-9 and his concerned gaze did offer solace. The next thing she knew she was dreaming of the months and years to come and picturing herself raising her daughter surrounded by puppies and kittens—and horses and cattle.

Shadow's deep bark brought her wide awake so suddenly she retained most of her dream and the initial few seconds of alertness were lovely. Then, she realized she was hearing the kind of canine warning that heralded trouble.

Swinging her feet off the bed Jamie rolled onto her side to push herself more erect. "What is it, boy? What's wrong?"

Footsteps thudded on the stairs. Ben was shouting, "Jamie."

She met him at the open door. "What is it? What's wrong?"

"We can't wait until morning after all. SAC Bridges just got word from an informant. The gang is preparing an assault."

"Here? On the ranch?"

"Yes." Entering the room he eyed her suitcases. "Are you packed?"

"Um, no. I guess I dozed off."

Instead of berating her he slung her bag onto the bed, opened it and held out both hands. "Toss everything you're going to need to me, and I'll do it."

"You're needed for defense, aren't you?"

"This is my job. You're my job. Now throw me your clothes or we'll leave without them."

"You're serious." It wasn't a question.

"Oh, yeah. Bridges figured we might have an hour, at best, before the shooting starts again."

"What about your dad? Mrs. E? And the ranch hands? We can't just abandon them."

"Once the gang gets word you're gone I expect them to try to follow us instead of laying siege to the Double S. The ones we leave behind will be much safer after we hit the road and I've asked the sheriff for temporary extra security."

"How will anyone know we're gone? We can't just wave a white flag and cruise down the highway, can we?"

"Good point," Ben said. He stepped away from the suitcase and headed for the door. "I'll give you five more minutes."

"Where are you going?"

"To arrange a decoy that should draw away anybody who's laying in wait. Dad can drive my truck and Mrs. E can pretend to be you and ride shotgun until they rendezvous with the sheriff's deputies. We'll take the Jeep, instead."

"Nobody will buy that trick," Jamie said, breathless and fighting dizziness. "Shadow won't be in your truck."

"No." She saw Ben cast a loving glance at his K-9 partner. "He's definitely going with us no matter what."

She was about to express thankfulness when Ben shouted, "Pack," and disappeared out the door.

FIFTEEN

Ben carried Jamie's bags down from the loft and stowed them in the rear of the Jeep, taking care to leave room for Shadow. A familiar truck was idling in front with Drew as driver.

He shook hands with his father. "Be careful, Dad."

Mrs. E leaned forward to speak past Drew. "We'll be fine. My hubby is meeting us a few miles away with our tractor. If he spots anybody following he'll force them off the road and hold them for the sheriff."

"Both of you, keep your heads down," Ben warned. "I don't want you getting hurt helping me."

"Helping you and that poor girl, you mean," Drew said. "I did the wrong thing years ago when I left Vi. Maybe this will kind of make up for it."

Ben laid a hand of comfort and support on

his dad's shoulder before stepping back. "Be careful."

Drew nodded soberly. "You, too."

Ben slapped the side of the truck with the flat of his hand in parting and ran back to Jamie. "Buckle up."

"I already have," she said. "I hope there were enough guns to go around."

Ben almost smiled at her. "This is the wilds of Wyoming. Trust me. We're well armed."

"Sorry." He saw her brace herself as he took off. "I guess I'm too much a city girl."

"You're fine. Hang on. I'm going to wait until my dad turns onto the highway, then follow a private ranch road to the northeast with my lights off, just in case. It may be bumpy in places because of the rain but I'll do my best to smooth it out for you." Noting the way she had pulled her coat close he asked, "Are you warm enough?"

"I will be when the heater kicks on. Right now I think I'm too scared to feel much."

"I *will* get you out of this," Ben vowed. "I know roads that aren't on any maps. We'll be in the clear in no time."

"I believe you."

He huffed. "You sound like you actually mean that."

It warmed his heart when she nodded and said, "I do."

* * *

As far as Jamie could tell they were hope-lessly lost.

At least she was. Every patch of sagebrush looked the same in the beams of the headlights that Ben had finally turned on and she'd quit gasping at every large shadowy object they passed because she couldn't tell what it was.

"Care to tell me why you picked this Jeep?"

"The camo paint and black canvas top will help hide us in a forest, plus this short wheel base makes it more maneuverable in all terrain."

"Logical. How about we call your dad and make sure he's okay? Just a real short check-in? Please?"

"I would like to know. Use my phone. It's on a protected line that should be undetectable."

"Really? There is such a thing?"

"Yes. I only got included in the network be-cause my unit is working with the FBI," Ben said. "The Feds have all kinds of neat toys."

"Guess so." She touched the screen, found the listing for Drew and connected quickly.

"Hi. How are you and Mrs. E?" Jamie asked.

The older man chuckled. "Last time I saw her, she had the drop on some yahoos in a fancy SUV and she and her husband were waiting for the sheriff."

"Good."

Ben partially turned his head. "Wait a minute. What number did you use?"

"The one you have programmed. Why?"

"Because I gave him a burner phone. Tell him we're fine and disconnect. Now."

"You heard Ben? We're fine." Her index finger was poised over the screen, ready to end the call. "Take care. If you can, text when you're sure nobody else is after you."

"Use the burner!" The shout from Ben covered whatever Drew said and she'd ended the call before the echo of it died down.

"I thought you said your line was secure," Jamie said.

"His cell isn't," Ben told her brusquely. "The less normal contact we have, the better."

"You could have said so in the first place."

"You didn't give me a chance."

"If you didn't want me to make the call, why did you offer me your phone?"

Ben's lack of response suggested that he was more upset at himself than at her. As a born peacemaker she yearned to reason with him, to somehow talk him out of his bad mood. She also knew that was not a good idea so she let the moment pass.

If her companion had been her ex instead of the cowboy cop, she wouldn't have even considered speaking up. Greg acted amiably around people he wanted to impress, but in private he often delivered scathing rebukes that made her cringe.

One more reason to be thankful he wasn't going to be in the baby's life, Jamie concluded. Matter of fact, she couldn't come up with a single reason to expose an innocent child to the kind of verbal abuse Greg loved to dish out.

What if he finds out and takes me to court? she wondered.

The mere notion of having to share custody gave her the shakes. Literally. Ben noticed. "You okay?"

"I'm fine. Why?"

"Because you just shivered or something. I thought you might still be cold."

"On the contrary," Jamie said. "I'm plenty warm."

He reached to turn down the heater, then paused and gave her a slight smile. "I hereby deputize you climate control officer. Set it to suit yourself."

Tempted to tease him, Jamie realized how moved she was to have been given control over the thermostat. Disrespect of her opinion had been a small thing in an ocean of small things, but each time Greg had criticized her choices she'd died a little inside. In retrospect she could see how his belittling had nearly destroyed her. And how standing up for herself had saved her at the last minute.

What had motivated her? It was hard to explain, even to herself. The phone call at night from a strange woman and his defensive reaction had certainly played a part, but the need to confirm her own worth had existed for a long time.

The road was leveling out so she was able to lean back and really relax for the first time since leaving the ranch. Tapping her trust in God, her love of His Son, Jesus, had given her what she'd needed to finally turn her cares and worries over to a higher power. In return, she had been able to see herself as a capable woman rather than one who needed Greg to run her life.

Jamie sighed. She liked the person she was becoming. No one was made instantly whole by faith, at least not in her experience, but she was growing in grace and intended to keep going until she'd proved her worth beyond a shadow of doubt.

Shadow. She began to smile and twisted a bit to look over her left shoulder. The Doberman's menacing image was totally reversed when she saw his pointy nose resting on Ben's shoulder, eyes nearly closed. She didn't blame him one bit. The few moments she'd spent leaning on that broad shoulder and trusting Ben's strength had been some of the best in memory.

"We're almost there," Ben said, pulling her mind back from its daydreaming. "Keep an eye out for a signpost."

"We made it? We got away?"

"It's looking good." Ben was fisting the wheel and leaning to peer into the dense foliage lining the curving mountain road. "Once we crossed Highway Fourteen we were pretty much home free."

"So where, exactly, are we going?"

"Have you ever heard of the Cloud Peak Wilderness area?"

Jamie felt her head begin to spin, her heart leaping as if she'd just received the shock of her life. Thinking she'd successfully hidden her negative reaction, she shrugged. "Maybe."

Ben was slowing the Jeep and pulling over as best he could on the narrow mountain trace that was barely a real road. "All right. Let's have it."

"Have what?"

"You know what I mean. You promised only the truth between us so tell me why you suddenly got so pale. Are you sick? You aren't having more contractions, are you?"

"No. It's not that," Jamie said. "I just didn't know where in Wyoming I was when I was at your ranch, so I never dreamed we'd be close to Cloud Peak." Pausing, she gathered her courage and tried to swallow past the cottony lump in her throat. "That's where Greg took me on our honeymoon."

Ben sighed, looking relieved. "It's a big wilderness area. Even if he happened to be in the neighborhood we'd never accidentally run into him. This cabin we're going to is way off the beaten track. I've only come up here a couple of times, myself."

Jamie bowed her head and stared at the baby bump beneath her coat. So much had happened since she'd been married that it seemed like a lifetime away.

But it wasn't, was it? The last few years of her adult life had been crammed with enough problems and woes and disappointments to fill a book but that didn't mean everything that happened to her had to be bad.

Peering at Ben through the drape of her silky hair she realized he was studying her, too. What did he want? Was he waiting for her okay to keep driving? Maybe. Probably.

"Well then, let's get a move on before sunrise catches us," she said, making an intense effort to lighten her tone and relieve his anxiety while stifling hers.

"I'm sorry to bring back unhappy memories."

Jamie shook her head. "Actually, the week I spent up here was one of the happiest of my life. The sad part was that it didn't last."

"You'll have plenty of time to make good memories in the future." He smiled. "With your little girl."

"From your lips to God's ears," she said, falling back on the old saying when nothing clever came to mind.

"Mine and my father's and Mrs. E's among others," Ben told her gently. "I told you a lot of people were praying for you."

Jamie was more than touched, she was overwhelmed with gratitude. Not many folks admitted to a strong prayer life and to have Ben mention it at that moment meant everything. Not only had she been sent away for protection, she'd been dropped right in the middle of a group of fellow Christians. She could not have asked for better.

The road to the cabin was so overgrown Ben almost missed his turn. Ruts in the drive tossed the Jeep to and fro while large rocks made it bump up and down more than usual. His main concern was his passenger. "I'm doing my best to keep it smooth. Are you okay?"

Although she was white-knuckling a hand-hold above her door, she shot him a lopsided smile. "Sure. I've always wanted to know how tennis shoes feel when they're bounced around in a clothes dryer."

He made a face at her. "I hope you're joking."

"You can't tell?" Jamie chuckled. "You know what they say. When a woman says she's *fine* and nothing else, that's the time to worry."

"I'll remember that." And he would. He'd remember everything about this smart, witty, sensitive young woman for as long as he lived. She was unique. Amazing in many ways, yet predictable in others. Having known her for such a short time, he assumed there was a lot more to her than the little he had discovered so far. Sadly, he'd probably never learn her whole story or experience the person she was when danger didn't threaten every moment of every day.

A particularly deep cut in the road canted the Jeep sideways, then righted it. Jamie squealed. "Whoa!"

"Sorry. We're almost there."

"No problem. I'm fine," she said, sounding breathless.

Ben immediately reacted. "Fine? What kind of fine? Your kind or the kind you just warned me about?"

She laughed. "My kind of truly okay. Pioneer wives bounced across the plains on wagon seats for months when they were expecting. The least I can do is tolerate a short ride to a cabin."

"Is that how you see yourself?" Ben asked. "As a pioneer?"

"In a way I suppose it is." She grew pensive, making him wonder if she was going to explain why. Finally, she said, "I'm a pioneer in my personal life. It's uncharted territory. I'm reinventing myself and trying to keep from making more mistakes while I do it."

"I get it."

"Do you? Have you ever felt like a total failure? No, I didn't think so. You were raised to be independent and stand tall. You were an army ranger once, too."

"How did you know that?"

Jamie shrugged. "I suppose somebody told me. There's more. You're a successful K-9 cop who manages to run a ranch in Wyoming and still work in Denver." She smiled over at him. "Shall I go on?"

"Feel free. I'm kind of enjoying this."

"Maybe later," Jamie said as she lifted her chin to indicate the bumpy road ahead. "You just drive."

"If you're at all uncomfortable we can stop

and rest," Ben offered. "This rough road can't be good for you or your baby."

"I've been uncomfortable for months," she said, laughing. "You men have no idea."

"I raise livestock. I have a pretty good grasp of the condition."

More laughter. "You don't have the slightest clue."

"Speaking of clues, have you given any more thought to the ring you photographed on the congresswoman's finger?"

"Beyond the fact she was messing around with my ex? Not really. Why?"

A heavy sigh and particularly tight turn in the narrow road gave him a good excuse to delay his reply while he considered the possible ramifications. "First, let me ask you something."

"Sure."

"You told me a little about Greg—that's his name, right?"

"Yes."

"Greg London."

"No. Not London. I took back my maiden name. Greg's is Jennings."

Ben's mind shifted into overdrive. He'd been through all the files pertaining to the gang that Hawkins, the killer, worked for but he'd been looking for anyone named London, not Jennings. It was such a common name he was afraid he might have read over it without remembering.

"One more question first." The wary look she gave him and her change in posture were evident even in the corner of his eye. "You said your ex didn't want you taking the job with the congresswoman. Is it possible he didn't know you were going to be near the scene of her murder that day?"

"Hold on a sec. Are you trying to blame *him*? I saw the killer with my own eyes. That's what got me into this mess in the first place." Her voice was rising, becoming strident.

"I know that. I just have all these details running around in my head and when you mentioned *clues* something clicked. Is there any chance your ex is mixed up in white collar crime? Natasha Clark had been chairing a committee investigating money laundering."

"No chance. He wasn't a crook, just a lousy husband."

Ben spotted the elusive cabin through the trees and breathed a sigh of relief. "Okay, okay. This is it. We'll talk more later."

All Jamie said in reply was, "Fine."

SIXTEEN

Jamie was through talking to Ben if he was going to be so unreasonable. It did feel odd, however, to be defending Greg to anyone, least of all the man designated to keep her alive to testify.

Ben parked, got out and circled to open her door. She slid to the ground with a muted groan and began to rub her back before she realized he was staring at her and frowning.

"I'm okay, all right. You don't have to watch me as though you expect me to explode any second."

"Sorry." Ben got her things out of the back of the Jeep, grabbed the bag he always kept ready and gave Shadow permission to jump down.

Jamie used the dog as a buffer. "Good boy, Shadow. Good boy."

"He needs to work right now," Ben told her. He called the K-9 to him, put the police vest on him and gave the command, "Patrol," followed by a sweep of his arm.

The quiet, seemingly empty forest around them suddenly took on a menace she hadn't noticed before. "You're scaring me."

"Good. Being complacent isn't smart. We need to be as alert as Shadow and twice as wise."

"We'll have to go some to beat that dog. He's amazing." She was afraid she might be overdoing the praise in the hope of getting back into Ben's good graces, but her comment about his canine partner came from the heart.

In what seemed like mere seconds the dog returned to Ben, panting and acting happy.

"Okay, we can go on in. He didn't smell anything out of the ordinary or he'd have stopped and barked."

"I can't believe how well he works. I mean, all you did was motion and he knew what to do."

Giving a slight bow and extending his arm toward the front door of the rustic cabin, Ben said nothing. When she took a few steps toward the porch he displayed a lopsided grin.

Jamie got the joke and laughed. "I take it I'm doing as well as the dog at reading your signs?"

"So far."

He followed her up the steps so closely it was unnerving. "You can back off. I've got this," she said. "I'm not an invalid, you know."

"I never said you were. Stand aside while I get the key."

"Oh, sorry." She gave him space. "Would it do any good to remind you that pregnant women have short tempers sometimes?"

"It might, as long as you don't tell me you're *fine* in that tone of voice again."

"Sorry. I'm really a nice person most of the time. I wish we'd met under more normal circumstances." That brought a laugh from Ben that surprised her. "What?"

He was shaking his head as he unlocked the door and preceded her. "This is normal for me. I almost never deal with people who aren't up to their necks in trouble. You're not nearly as bad as some."

"Thanks, I think."

A musty odor made the small cabin seem uninviting, but Jamie entered without negative comment. He'd warned her that the place hadn't been occupied, so it stood to reason it would be dusty and dank and a little moldy. At least she didn't smell mice.

While Shadow sniffed every nook and cranny, Ben tossed his heavy go-bag onto a small table and busied himself checking the windows and other door. "I'd tell you to sit down but that's probably not a good idea until I've had a chance to lay something clean over the sofa and chairs and wipe down the flat surfaces."

She nodded, more than willing to let him take charge in this case. "Fine. Sorry, I mean *great*." Jamie smiled at him. "I wouldn't know where to start."

Watching him open one of four plastic totes stacked in the corner of the single room, she realized he'd done this before. His movements were efficient and his prime physical condition was more than evident. It was a joy to observe. Not that she noticed, of course.

That errant thought made her blush. Because the room had only two doors that she could see, she assumed the restroom was through the second one. It had better be.

When she opened that door, however, her biggest worry was confirmed. No indoor plumbing. She groaned.

"What's the matter?"

Making a face at him she said, "I'll need to borrow a flashlight."

His brows arched. "Ah. I'll walk you out."

"No need."

"What will you do if you stumble on a hibernating rattle snake and his buddies? Do you think they'll just calmly slither aside for you?"

"They might if I asked nicely."

The way he drawled, "*Riiiight*," deserved the slight smile she gave him.

"We'll all go," Jamie countered, determined to end this ridiculous standoff. "C'mon, Shadow."

With the K-9 in the lead and Ben following, Jamie tagged along at the end of the line. The ground was slippery with half melted snow and ice left over from the last storm. Spring was coming later in the high country than it had at the Sawyer ranch.

"This path is slippery. Take my hand," Ben said.

Pride told her to refuse. Common sense caused her to accept his offer. "Thanks."

With her free arm extended, Jamie tried to balance despite the uneven, slick surface. "I feel like a tightrope walker."

Ben laughed and glanced back at her. "You look like one, too."

She saw the protruding tree root seconds before the toe of his cowboy boot caught in it. She tried to pull her hand free but he was holding too tightly. There was only one thing to do. Brace herself and lean against the fall he was about to take. "Look out."

"What?" Too late to stop himself he took that fateful step.

Jamie pulled the opposite direction. Ben released his hold on her, arms cartwheeling, as he fought for balance.

It was as if everything was happening in slow motion. She staggered back, encountered a tree and hugged it. Ben took a couple of steps forward, then back, then sideways before he landed in a pile of slushy snow.

Giggles bubbled up. She covered her mouth to stifle them until he bounced to his feet, unhurt. After that, it was no use.

"I'm glad you're amused," he grumbled.

"Sorry. I'm afraid I may be a tad keyed up. I used to get the giggles like this when I was a kid."

"Yeah, well, I'll check for snakes."

Jamie was still grinning at him when he handed her the light. "You never told me you could dance."

Ben enjoyed seeing her laugh even if it was at him. Not only had she been far too serious most of the time, her smile lit her pretty face and made those green eyes twinkle like stars. Did she know how beautiful she was? He doubted it. Considering the kind of marriage she'd had, it was a wonder she had as much spunk left as she did.

Should he wait for her or would that undermine her confidence? he wondered. Stepping off the path onto the drifts of dead leaves gave him much better footing for the descent and he chastised himself for not thinking of that before.

Rising sun behind the ridge to the east was beginning to light the forest. He cupped a hand around his mouth and called, "I'm leaving Shadow to guard you and heading back. The ground next to the path isn't as slippery. Walk down that way and you'll be fine."

A muted "Fine" made him smile and shake his head, picturing Jamie's face all the way back to the cabin.

Working her way down the slight incline with the K-9 at her side, Jamie couldn't help seeing the blessing in her present situation. The forest was beautiful. Backlighted by a pinkish sky and dripping with morning dew it was so perfect it almost brought her to tears.

Sniffling and redirecting her thoughts ended that. One idea she did have trouble banishing was how much she truly cared for the cowboy cop. Logic insisted he was merely doing his job. A sense of hope, of impossible possibilities, kept disagreeing. It was more than his duty. It had to be. No one would be that nice, that accommodating, that concerned and gentle if he didn't have some tender feelings for her.

"There goes my imagination again," Jamie told the faithful K-9. Shadow panted a sweet doggie smile back at her. "Not only am I getting silly about your partner, I'm taking the chance of falling in love. I don't want to repeat the mistake I made once and consider marriage again, so I'm really stuck. Let's face it, boy, I do not understand men. Or life."

Shadow's single bark struck her as the reply of a friend and made her smile again.

The rear cabin door was standing open. Ben had been watching. Blushing, Jamie sincerely hoped he hadn't overheard her one-sided conversation.

"Airing the place out?"

"Keeping an eye on you."

She passed him the flashlight. "Thanks. You were right about the leaves next to the path."

"You're just now deciding I'm always right?"

"Who said anything about *always*?" As she'd hoped, he laughed and the sound touched her every nerve, making her wonder if he had sensed a change in their nonexistent relationship. Had she been as truly brave as she envisioned herself, she might have asked him. Perhaps she still would, eventually. Once she'd testified and her special protection ended would be a good time.

Entering the cabin, she noticed how much cleaner it looked. "Hey. Almost livable."

"Thanks, I think. There's no running water but my friend keeps big jugs for washing up and things. There's a pan of sudsy water over there in the sink."

"What about heat?"

"The wood-burning stove does double duty. As soon as I bring in some wood and fire it up it'll probably be so warm in here we'll want to leave the doors open all day."

"Is that safe?"

"With Shadow on the job it is. He'll hear if anybody gets near and alert us."

"What would we do without him, huh?"

The fond expression on Ben's face, the warmth in his gaze as he looked at his K-9, was unmistakable. He loved that dog the way most people loved family and friends. Jamie could easily understand why. As part of the Rocky Mountain K-9 Unit, the name embroidered on his working vest, Shadow was more than special. He was irreplaceable. Especially to Ben Sawyer.

Jamie wanted to tell Ben how much she appreciated his protection, how glad she was that she'd been sent to him in Wyoming instead of anywhere else. Unfortunately, the more she thought about what to say, the more choked up she got. It would not do for him to think she was a crybaby. When everything was over she'd thank him. Properly but with restrained dignity.

Kiss his cheek? The mere notion brought redness and warmth to her face. *I am certifiable,* she told herself. *My mind has turned this normal man into some kind of superhero.*

She sighed heavily. Right or wrong, she'd mentally elevated Ben to a higher status. Was that why she kept seeing him as so special, so wonderful? Probably so. Given his job and her need for protection, however, considering him totally capable and trusting him completely was comforting.

Relaxed enough to start to doze off, Jamie jumped when Shadow unexpectedly barked.

Ben was on his feet in a heartbeat, gun drawn. "Shut the back door and lock it!"

Jamie pushed herself off the overly soft sofa and did her best to hurry.

Ben ran the opposite direction, following his partner.

She twisted the dead bolt and spun around. A

quick look told her one irrefutable thing. There was no place to hide in the rustic cabin. If her enemies came through the door, she'd be a sitting duck.

SEVENTEEN

Gripping his gun with both hands, Ben pivoted around the doorjamb and onto the front porch to scan the surrounding territory. Shadow stood on the top step, barking at something he'd apparently spotted through the trees.

Ben remained cautious. His dog was trained to not react to other animals, but he'd never taken him this deep into the wilds before. Therefore, it was slightly possible he might be barking at a deer or an elk. Possible, not probable.

A few steps took Ben to the edge of the wooden porch. "What is it, Shadow?"

White tails bounded away in the distance, showing Ben what had likely triggered the barking.

The K-9 kept shifting his paws as if he wanted to bolt. "No. No chasing deer," Ben said in a warning tone. In normal circumstances he'd leash his dog and they'd make certain that the deer were the only cause for alarm, but he couldn't leave Jamie alone. And he certainly couldn't take her along on a possible manhunt.

Finally, Shadow settled down. That was a relief. It was unlikely that anyone had traced them to this hideaway.

As his pulse slowed and his nerves stopped firing wildly, Ben backed into the cabin and commanded Shadow to come with him.

"Did you see anybody?" Jamie asked.

Ben frowned. "No. Where are you?"

She rose from behind the sofa. "Hiding. There aren't many good places in here."

"You did okay. Hungry?" He holstered his gun and smiled.

"Famished. What's on the menu?"

"Nothing hot, I'm afraid, until I build a fire in the stove. Do you want to wait for breakfast or have a snack now?"

"If you don't want me fighting your dog for his treats, it would be a good idea to feed me sooner rather than later."

"Granola bar or power bar?"

Jamie grinned and held out her hands. "Both."

Laughing, he dug in a side pocket of his canvas bag and brought out a handful of emergency hikers' rations. "I have trail mix, too. Is chocolate all right for babies?"

"This one loves it," Jamie assured him. "She told me."

"Oh, she did, did she? How?"

"That's a secret between me and her." Jamie held up the trail mix. "You're sure you don't mind?"

"Pace yourself," Ben said with a smile. "This bag only holds what I need for several days if I'm called away on an assignment and don't have time to pack."

"Meaning, enough for one but not for two and a half."

"Something like that." He started for the rear door. "Will you be okay if I go outside for firewood?"

"Sure. But do we need a fire now? You could save the wood for tonight, when the temperature drops again."

"That depends. Do you like cold Spam?"

The way she wrinkled up her nose made him chuckle. "Okay. Stay in here with Shadow. The woodpile is just off the porch back here. It won't take me a minute."

Extra caution slowed Ben down. Still he was only outside for a few minutes. When he returned, Jamie was sound asleep on the sofa. Her coat was pulled tight and next to her lay the empty water bottle and a severely depleted bag of trail mix.

Poor thing. She was a trouper all right, but she was also human. Repeated surges of adrenaline were enough to tire out the strongest man. This young pregnant woman had undergone that same test of stamina and had held out until now. No wonder she'd fallen asleep so fast.

He reached into the open canvas bag and unfolded the thin silver insulating cover he'd brought with them. Laying it over Jamie didn't wake her, probably because it was very lightweight and she was so exhausted.

What he wanted to do was tuck it in around her, smooth the hair off her forehead and lean down to give her a whisper of a kiss. Instead, he straightened and stepped back, watching her breathe and marveling at the child beneath the blanket with her. He'd never really given babies much thought. Children, yes, particularly the waifs he'd tried to help while overseas. But a baby was a whole different thing. It was tiny. Helpless. Completely dependent upon adults to care for it. To love it.

How did a single mother cope? It had to be terribly difficult, as Chris had said when he'd told Ben some details about his childhood. No wonder the guy was bitter. Chris loved his own mother and would naturally be defensive of her when it came to Drew walking away to marry another woman. That was a reaction Ben could understand better after having met Jamie. Perhaps the key was going to be getting Chris to believe that Drew had been clueless until many years had passed, when it was too late to go back and become the father Chris had needed.

His cell phone vibrated. He checked to see why. A text from Drew had arrived, thankfully via the burner phone. All it said was, Bad guys arrested, good guys ready for a nap. Ben snorted quietly, then blocked their number so they wouldn't be able to get in touch again, just in case. If they had been dealing with a run-of-the-mill street gang there would be less reason for concern. Too bad the men who had ordered the Natasha Clark murder were anything but ordinary.

Ben got himself another bottle of water, settled down in a chair and simply watched Jamie sleep. To his chagrin, this assignment had already morphed into a whole lot more than he'd expected. And it wasn't over yet.

Jamie had napped so long she was positive she wouldn't sleep a wink when night fell. Her body fooled her. She slept like the proverbial baby and wouldn't have roused nearly as often if her real baby hadn't been practicing tap dancing while doing a handstand. At least that's what it had felt like.

She yawned, raking her fingers through her hair. Ben was at the woodstove, frying something in a pan. That didn't interest her nearly as much as the coffee she could smell.

"Good morning," he said amiably.

"Um. Morning. I should remind you, I'm not at my best until I've had my coffee."

"Coming up." He poured her a mug and delivered it to the sofa.

"Thanks. What's new?"

"I told you last night when you briefly woke up that Dad and Mrs. E and her husband were fine, didn't I?"

"Yes." She took a sip and burned her tongue. "Ouch. Hot."

"Sorry. There's no temperature control on a woodstove, just a damper. A cook has to have a lot of practice to control the rate of burning."

"Another thing to praise the pioneer wives for."

"Agreed. I'd ask if you slept well but I know you did. I was watching you."

"All night?" She was dumbfounded. "Didn't you sleep?"

"Some. I've learned to doze in a chair. It's a helpful skill if you don't have a chance to climb into bed."

"Doesn't your friend have a place to sleep here?"

Jamie felt even worse about keeping Ben up when he said, "Yes. You were using it."

"I'm so sorry. I didn't mean to take over like that. Tonight I'll nap in the chair and you can have the sofa."

"Not necessary."

Jamie was adamant. "No. I mean it. I nap in a recliner at home. Makes it easier to breathe." The quizzical look on his face almost made her laugh again. "You've never thought of that?"

"Can't say I have. The mares and heifers have never shown breathing problems."

"Well, now you know. It's not all the time, just when my passenger decides to redecorate her temporary home. There are times when it feels like she's hammering nails into the walls to hang pictures." Jamie smiled at the memory. "Last night I'm sure she was taking dance lessons in there."

Ben had poured himself a mug of coffee. He set the frying pan aside and joined her on the couch. "Know what amazes me?"

"What?"

Had she been expecting him to get serious, she wouldn't have been so surprised when he said, "You."

"Me?"

"Yes." Nodding, he took another sip. "You seem so calm about it all. I find that amazing."

"It's helped that I've educated myself about what to expect. Besides, once you're in, you're in." Mug in one hand, she laid her other hand on the baby bump as if she was stroking an infant she could see. "It's not her fault she had a louse for a father. The only thing that worries me is Greg's possible change of heart in the future. I don't want him to have anything to do with me or his daughter."

"I suspect that's how my half brother's mom felt," Ben said. "My father had no idea Vi was expecting when he married my mom. I don't know what he'd have done if he'd found out."

"That's too bad."

"For them, yes. It saved my mother from a terrible heartache."

"What did she say when she found out?"

Ben was shaking his head and staring into his steaming coffee. "She never knew. She passed away before Chris came looking for our dad."

"What a sad story. No wonder your father broods. Is that why you feel you need to spend so much time at the ranch?"

"Part of it," Ben told her. "Drew's been slipping mentally, emotionally. I try to keep the Double S running in the hopes he'll recover his faculties and be able to manage more without me some day."

"What do doctors say?"

"My opinion? The ones he's seen don't have a clue. There are no solid tests like finding indicators in the blood to pin down forms of dementia so it's basically objective."

"I'm sorry. Admittedly I don't know him well, but I do think he looked and acted better when he came running into the barn to tell you those cattle had been slaughtered."

She was glad to see Ben's mood visibly brighten. "He did, didn't he? His problem comes and goes. Are you ready for your fried Spam and powdered scrambled eggs?"

The thought of eating such a heavy meal comprised of adulterated food was not at all appealing. The idea of refusing the meal Ben had prepared for her was equally unacceptable. "Sure. Got any ketchup?"

"No gourmet chef would permit you to cover his masterpiece with that stuff."

"I agree." Jamie giggled. "So, got any ketchup?"

"If I say no?"

"Then I'll choke it down some way. And when we leave here I'll mail your friend a couple of bottles for the next poor, hungry traveler." She accepted the paper plate he handed her. "How long do you think we'll have to stay here, anyway?"

"No way to predict. As long as…"

Shadow got to his feet, muscles rippling beneath his sleek coat. A growl rumbled. His upper lip curled.

Jamie froze, plate in one hand, a fork in the other.

Ben was on his feet and drawing his gun. "Behind the couch. Now."

Her food hit the floor as she bolted for cover. "You said nobody followed us. Maybe it's just a lost hiker or something."

"I hope so." He was peering out the window while standing off to one side to stay out of sight. "I don't see anybody yet."

"Maybe it's a herd of deer."

"Shadow barked at the deer, he didn't growl. Whatever it is, my partner thinks it's a threat."

"Is his judgment that fine-tuned?"

"More so than my own," Ben said. "Stay put. Don't come outside no matter what you think you hear until I come back for you."

That plan seemed fairly sensible until Jamie thought more about it. Suppose something happened to Ben? Suppose he got hurt or captured? What would she do then?

"Don't leave. Please."

Ben seemed to be considering her plea. Then he bolted out the door without a word. Jamie heard the Jeep door slam. Boots thudded on the wooden porch.

He thrust a small cardboard box of .12 gauge shells at her. "Do you remember how to load?"

Of course! The shotgun. He'd brought it in with their other supplies and was now giving her extra ammunition. Jamie nodded rapidly. "Yes."

"Okay. Load and get ready. Just don't shoot unless you're sure of your target and positive it isn't me."

"What about other people?"

"That'll be up to you and Shadow," Ben said. "I'm leaving him here with you. If his teeth can't hold off an attacker, shoot."

"I don't think I can…" His gaze had drifted to her torso and she read the caution in his eyes.

"I'll do what I have to and no more," Jamie vowed. "Make sure you come back."

Ben slipped a lanyard around his neck with his badge and ID attached, then squared a police-department baseball cap on his head. "Make sure you don't accidentally shoot me when I do."

EIGHTEEN

Sunlight filtering through the trees gave the forest a dappled appearance and helped camouflage anything that didn't move. Ben took up a position up a hill behind the cabin so he could observe both doors at the same time. If anybody came for Jamie he'd be ready.

"I miss you, Shadow," he whispered to himself, cautious because he knew how well sound carried across the hills and valleys. Somewhere, a woodpecker was beating a cadence looking for a meal hidden in the trunk of a tree. Squirrels chattered and leaped from branch to branch, noisily upset that he had invaded their territory. Small birds sang, called, squawked and flitted overhead.

Moving slowly, evenly, Ben raised his binoculars. Anyone he could see could see him, too. Stealth was paramount.

At first, nothing. Then a glint. There and

gone. He froze, concentrating on the direction it had come from. There it was again, not as prominent as the flash from the SUV had been back at his ranch but there, nonetheless. Perhaps sunlight hitting the lens of binoculars or a spotting scope and bouncing off?

Pinpointing the area where the flash had originated, Ben started to circle around. If whoever it was stayed put just a few minutes longer he'd have them.

Moisture on the fallen leaves muffled his footsteps. True to his innate sense of direction he wove through the underbrush, keeping larger objects between him and his goal. Every time he advanced he paused for a few moments to listen. Nothing.

The closer he got to the place he'd seen the flash, the harder his heart pounded. He finally drew his gun again, glad he was armed yet wishing he'd brought the more imposing-looking shotgun. Jamie was one of the only people he'd ever trusted to master a long gun as fast as she had. Of course, she was also the only one he'd taught who had such a compelling reason to want to learn.

Gripping the pistol with both hands, Ben raised it. Instinct and keen hearing insisted the person he wanted to confront was just ahead. If he was wrong, he was about to blow his cover. If he was right, he might be closing in on the key to who was after Jamie London.

In a fluid motion, he pivoted around the tree, braced himself and brought his sidearm to bear on a heavyset man wearing camo clothing. "Freeze. Police."

The watcher didn't jump the way most people would have. Slowly and purposely he let the binoculars swing free and raised both hands. "Hey, man, I'm just birdwatching."

"Yeah right." Ben didn't lower his gun.

"Okay, okay. I admit it," the man drawled. "I was scoutin' for a big buck I spotted a week or so ago."

"It's not hunting season."

Camo-covered shoulders shrugged. The man's hands began to drop lower and lower.

"Hands up. And keep 'em there."

Still, the watcher kept up the ruse. "Hey, man, I'm tellin' you the truth."

"Yeah? You alone?"

"'Course I am."

"Turn around with your back to me and put your hands on your head."

Movement was slow and controlled, setting Ben's nerves on edge even more. "Feet apart. Fingers laced together."

Ben had no doubt this trespasser was familiar with the usual procedure because he never missed a beat. This was the tricky part for an arresting officer working without backup, the approach and cuffing. This was the moment when so much could go wrong if the suspect chose to resist.

Without holstering his gun, Ben pulled out a plastic zip tie. "Okay. Hands behind you. And no funny moves.

"You're gonna be sorry for this," camo man threatened.

There. That was what Ben had been waiting for, the emergence of this man's true character. All the evidence now agreed. He was no birdwatcher or law-breaking hunter. He was exactly what he looked like—a thug sent to harm the federal witness so she couldn't or wouldn't testify.

The wary criminal did all he could to make fastening the tie difficult but Ben persevered. He was about to march him back to the cabin and do a better job of securing his wrists with Shadow there as backup when the perp suddenly threw his bulky body backward.

One broad shoulder caught Ben full in the chest and knocked him down. Before he could catch his breath his perp was running through the forest, dodging trees and occasionally stumbling over rough terrain.

"Stop! Or I'll shoot."

When the camo-clad figure kept going, Ben fired a warning shot into the air.

The man's pace slowed but he didn't stop.

Ben shot again, this time into the ground. He'd already made up his mind that the next time he pulled the trigger he'd be aiming higher, but it wasn't necessary.

The big man dropped to his knees, able to raise both hands over his head because he'd worked free of the restraint. "Okay, okay, no need to go all Western on me."

"Put both hands together in front of you and use your teeth to pull the zip tie."

"Yuck. I could sue you for cruel and unusual punishment."

"You can do whatever you want to later. Right now, you're going to put that tie around both wrists. And don't try anything else. Got that?"

"Yeah, yeah, I've got it."

As soon as the thug complied Ben closed the distance between them. The blow to his chest had reminded him of being tackled by a linebacker in a football game. Hopefully, his remaining shortness of breath was due to the excitement rather than a bruised or broken rib. He couldn't afford to show weakness of any kind.

Ben straight-armed the thug's back. "Let's go."

"Go where?"

"To that cabin you were watching."

"What cabin? I told you. I was looking for birds."

"Pardon me if I don't buy that. I know what's going on." Another push kept his captive moving.

"Do you? I doubt it." A smirk accompanied that remark and left Ben decidedly unsettled. Moreover, muscles in his side were beginning to spasm.

One thing was certain. As soon as he got back to Jamie they were going to run. If no stationary location was secure, then they'd keep driving until the FBI picked them up and ended this.

God willing I'll be able to save her, Ben thought to himself, turning it into a silent prayer. *Father, help us both.*

When Jamie saw Ben coming with his prisoner she cradled the loaded shotgun in her arms like a baby, checked the nearby areas by sight, then stepped out onto the porch. It didn't surprise her when he yelled, "Pack."

That was an order her heart and mind insisted she heed. Not only did she step back to avoid the creepy-looking guy Ben had in custody, she wanted to give him plenty of room to maneuver.

The two men passed her. Ben told Shadow, "Guard," then pointed to a straight chair and spoke to the other man, "You. Park it." If the guy hadn't been smiling when he sat down she would have felt much better about his presence.

"In my bag," Ben said, pointing first to Jamie, then to the object. "The black zip ties are the longest. Grab some of them and fasten our guest to this chair."

Jamie was more than happy to obey. Circling the chair with a handful of ties, she was glad the dog was so well trained because getting this close to the burly man was scary. His wrist tie looked loose, so she redid that one right away, then looked to Ben for approval.

"Good. He got loose once and I don't intend to let him do it again."

"Why didn't you just tie him to a tree or something?"

"Because I want to talk to him while you get ready. Finish that and start packing survival supplies. Don't forget to strap his ankles to the legs of the chair."

Determined to say or do nothing that might

undermine Ben's authority she decided to not mention the frailty of the old wooden chair. As she worked she was watching Ben, too. There seemed to be a change in the way he moved, a lack of ease in his posture as he rested, perched on the arm of the sofa, yet she knew better than to ask.

"We're not taking him with us, are we?"

"No. I'll leave him here for law enforcement."

"What if…" Jamie broke off when she caught Ben's warning glance. The lack of a foolproof way to secure their prisoner had not escaped the K-9 cop and without Shadow on duty she doubted he'd have brought the danger so close to her.

Once she got the hang of positioning and tightening the ties, she finished quickly, straightened to rub her lower back and retreated. "Done?"

"Looks good." He still hadn't holstered his gun even though the K-9 was also standing guard.

"Want me to grab your stuff, too?"

Ben nodded. "Please. And Shadow's bowls. Once we hit the road I plan to keep going for as long as necessary."

The thug in the chair still looked amused. "Won't do you any good. I've already radioed your position and a description of your Jeep to my friends. You and the woman are dead meat." He snorted. "The mutt, too."

"And who might *they* be?" Ben asked, surprising Jamie with the nonchalance of his delivery. "I always like to know who's trying to kill me."

"You already know unless you're dumber than you look."

"Oh, yeah? Maybe I'm wrong. Want to prove it one way or another?"

Jamie kept packing although she momentarily held her breath. For a few seconds she thought Ben's efforts might fail until the man said, "Let me put it this way. Your girlfriend won't be doing any testifying in court."

So, it was all about the Hawkins trial as they'd thought from the beginning. That was little comfort.

The baby kicked. Jamie's strained back ached. The food she had eaten was rolling around in her upset stomach and she was getting a little dizzy.

Breathe came to mind and she inhaled sharply, drawing Ben's attention and an arch of his eyebrows, so she made an okay sign with her fingers.

The last of their getaway supplies were packed. Jamie straightened, ignoring the pain in her lower back. That sensation wasn't new.

Changes in her body and center of balance had brought it on before, more times than she could count.

She watched Ben start to rise. Saw him flinch. Tried to ask him what was wrong via her eyes and facial expression.

He didn't comment but their captive did.

"Aw, sorry," the thug said. "Did I hit you too hard? Break a rib, maybe?"

The lack of rebuttal from Ben truly worried her. As soon as they were on the road and away from this awful man she intended to insist on hearing the whole story. For now, though, she would simply help him load the Jeep.

"I'll get all that," Ben said flatly. "You go wait outside."

"I can carry some."

"Take your camera bag and go get in the Jeep. I'll bring the rest." He holstered his gun and started forward.

"Really, I can…"

He was close enough in three strides to set her heart on fire and make her unsteady. When he leaned over to whisper in her ear it took every ounce of control Jamie could muster to keep from closing her eyes and pressing her cheek to his.

"Go get in the Jeep." Ben grasped her hand and pressed a set of keys into it. "Driver's seat.

If you see or hear anything out of the ordinary, start the engine and drive away as fast as you can."

She was shaking her head. His breath was warm against her face and she felt Ben gently tuck her hair behind her ear before continuing, "Promise."

"No," was barely audible.

"That's an order," Ben said.

"Why?"

He briefly glanced at the thug. "Because we don't know how far away his reinforcements were when he told them about us."

"Then we'd better get a move on," Jamie declared, stepping away to scoop up both her camera equipment and one of the bags she'd just packed. "Come on."

"Listen" was all she permitted before countering. "No, you listen. It's me they're after and if you think I'm reckless enough to hit the road without you and Shadow you'd better think again. This is my life we're talking about and it's my fault we're all in danger. Now stop arguing and follow me."

The menacing laughter coming from the man tied to the chair made the tiny hairs on Jamie's arms and at the nape of her neck bristle, but she didn't let that deter her.

"Don't go out there without a gun!" Ben shouted.

Had she thought of taking the shotgun with her to start with she might have grabbed it. Since it currently lay across the table, she'd get it on her second trip. Or her third, depending on how badly Ben was hurt and how much he could carry.

The door stood open when she returned from the Jeep and she passed her injured guardian in the doorway. His teeth were gritted but he was toting everything she'd left behind.

Jamie hurried back and opened the Jeep for him. As soon as he was secure in the passenger seat he whistled, and Shadow came barreling out of the cabin.

By the time she reached the driver's door the K-9 had leaped over his human partner and was waiting in the rear with the baggage while Ben rode shotgun. Literally. The window was rolled down on his side of the cab and he had the barrel of the shotgun resting on the sill.

NINETEEN

"We'll have to backtrack a little," Ben said. "It'll be bumpy."

"This isn't your fault."

Although she was driving cautiously his ribs were still complaining. "Unless the bouncing around bothers you, this is a good time to drive faster."

"Actually, holding on to the steering wheel helps. I feel much less like those tennis shoes I mentioned."

"Terrific." By crossing his arms and pressing his elbows to his sides, Ben was able to steady the shotgun and support his sore side. It was past time to report their situation to his head-quarters, so he did.

"This is Sawyer, RMKU. Cell service is spotty up here so I'll make this fast," Ben said as soon as he connected. "Our cover is blown. We're headed northwest from Cloud Peak in a camo-painted Jeep with a black rag top. I'll leave this phone on so the FBI can track it and come and get us. The sooner my witness is secure the better." Static filled the connection before it failed.

He glanced at Jamie. One eyebrow was raised in an unspoken question. Ben shook his head. "I have to assume they got all that. We lost the signal before I was able to confirm." He paused to study her, puzzled. Understanding her current expression was like trying to read a book with the cover closed.

The tires bumped through a pothole. Ben winced and bit back a wordless sound of pain. That broke the silence.

"So, what happened out there in the woods?" Jamie asked. "That guy said he hit you. Is that how you got hurt?"

Denial was futile. "Yeah. He must have played a lot of football as a kid because his shoulder sure packed a punch."

"Is there anything I can do to help you?"

"You're doing it," Ben said flatly. "As soon as we hit the highway I'll take over."

"Oh, you don't like my driving?"

"It's not your steering that's lacking, it's your foot on the gas pedal. There's no lead in it."

"I'm not in any hurry to join my ancestors and meet Jesus, if that's what you're saying. I either trust God or I don't." Her smile blossomed. "I was just thinking how nice it would be if we had a dozen trained attack K-9s like Shadow. Then we could sit back and let them do all the work."

"What happened to the woman who was afraid of dogs a few days ago?"

"Haven't seen her lately," Jamie teased. "She's learned a lot since coming to your ranch."

"Did you like it there?" The question had to be asked. His heart insisted. And when Jamie nodded he breathed so deeply it cramped his side again.

"Actually, I loved it. Except the part about falling off the fence during a stampede. Oh, and being shot at."

"What about the drone?"

She chuckled. "That part was fun."

"You'd never be able to make that shot again if you tried," he taunted, positive she'd have a snappy comeback.

"Let's hope I never have to try unless we're just practicing."

Something about the way she was talking gave him the idea she wanted to return to the Double S, so he said, "You're welcome to come visit Wyoming anytime, whether I'm there or not. You know we have plenty of room at the ranch."

"I would love to see that sweet mare's foal when it's born. Of course, I may have a baby of my own to cramp my style by the time she has hers."

"Babies are portable," Ben reminded her, wishing he'd had more time to get to know Jamie and for her to see more of what made him tick. Truth to tell, he wanted to see her daughter as a newborn, maybe even hold her. That was a new emotion for him and one that was pretty scary, considering his previously negative opinion about marriage and children.

She laughed. "I suppose they are. I'll be glad to be able to put this one down in a crib after toting her around for months."

"You still feeling okay?"

"Sure." Flexing her shoulders and stretching against the seat belt, she made a soft moaning sound that was barely audible above the roar of the engine.

Watching her from the corner of his eye, Ben saw Shadow react by laying his head on her shoulder. It would have been kind of cute if it hadn't been a clear sign that the K-9 was instinctively as concerned about her as he was.

They turned onto a paved road in less than a half hour. No one had pursued them so far and Ben felt comfortable telling Jamie to stop. "It's time to switch drivers."

"Are you sure?"

"Positive. Pull over."

Slowing, she eased the Jeep off the road onto the gravel shoulder. "We should tape up your ribs."

"Later." He propped the shotgun between them with the safety on so it wouldn't be dangerous. Despite the stabbing pains in his side he still made it around the vehicle before Jamie had swiveled to slide out, so he lifted his arms to catch her.

"I can manage."

"I know you can. I'm just trying to help."

Halfway through saying, "I don't need..." she slipped and dropped the final few inches. Ben caught her without gasping in pain, sensing a difference in their embrace and wondering why. He suspected it might be because he'd never really hugged a woman in Jamie's condition before, which might be the reason he wanted to scoop her up in his arms and carry her to the passenger side.

He resisted. She briefly laid her forehead against his chest before pulling away. "Thanks. I'm okay. Let's roll."

"Let me get that other door for you."

It didn't surprise him one bit when she made a face. "Nonsense. Get in and get ready. I'll take care of myself."

He wanted to remind her she had needed him only moments before but chose to pass up the chance. Self-confidence was good for her. The less she leaned on him or anyone else, the better, at least until she'd testified and this threat had passed. There would surely be times he wasn't able to be with her, and she needed to be as cautious and self-sufficient as possible.

The effort to twist far enough to click the buckle on his seat belt was excruciating. Ben noticed that Jamie seemed to be having equal problems so he reached over. "I'll fasten yours if you'll fasten mine," he said with a lopsided smile. "I seem to be as much in need as you are."

Luminous green eyes twinkled. Jamie grinned. "Since you put it that way, cowboy, okay."

"I'm in cop mode now," Ben said, fixing her belt, then leaning back so she could assist him with his. "No more cowboy."

"I wondered why you'd ditched the Stetson for a ball cap."

"Police logo," he said, glancing at his side mirror before pulling back onto the highway. Traffic was sparse and the closest oncoming vehicle looked at least a quarter of a mile away.

Jamie, too, was checking the large exterior mirror. "Am I seeing things or does that SUV back there look familiar?"

"Don't worry. There are hundreds on the road just like it."

"Yes, but, I imagine our prisoner's buddies drive the same kind of vehicle you kept seeing on the ranch, don't you?"

"If they were smart they wouldn't." What he didn't tell her was that thugs in a criminal organization as large and powerful as the one Hawkins worked for would be far less likely to worry about masking their identity. They didn't care who knew what they were up to because they figured to escape prosecution, just as Hawkins expected to by having Jamie London killed before she could testify.

Ben stomped on the gas. Accelerating up a hill, he kept watch on the sparse traffic behind, noting that his speed was sufficient to visibly widen the distance. The real question was how had they been trailed so easily in the first place? *Could* there be a leak at the RMK9 Unit or in the FBI? Whoever had sabotaged the ammo for the training demonstration that had hurt Shadow last month was probably still working undercover within the police department. Perhaps it was someone in his unit, although each man and K-9 pair had been thoroughly vetted.

"No. It can't be one of them," Ben muttered. He knew each man in his group, some from even before Tyson had formed the K-9 unit, and there wasn't one he didn't trust implicitly, even his disgruntled half brother. Men and women who handled K-9s were different from most regular cops. They had to be to work efficiently with their dogs. The ability to sense an animal's mood was instinctive and couldn't be taught. Honing that skill while working with a trainer was the second step. Total trust in their K-9 partner was the final one. Not one of them would allow one of their dogs to be harmed. Even accidentally.

Ben checked all the mirrors again. The center one reflected the smiling face of Shadow, tongue hanging from his mouth, watching the road ahead. There had been human partners he hadn't trusted as much as he trusted that amazing K-9. To say he loved that furry face and the look of intelligence in those deep brown eyes was no exaggeration. Not that he would have admitted it to anyone other than himself.

"Why are you smiling?" Jamie asked.

"Just thinking about my special friend in the back seat."

"You mean my hero?"

It occurred to Ben to counter that *he* wanted to be her hero, but he quickly pushed down that urge. Instead, he said, "Yup. He's mine, too."

* * *

Sunlight through the windows of the Jeep bathed Jamie's face with warmth and made her sleepy. She yawned behind her hand.

"Am I boring you?" Ben asked.

"Better to be bored than scared witless."

"You do have a point there."

"How much farther?"

"What do you mean?"

"Where are we going? You must have some idea."

"Nope."

It bothered her to see him smiling. "I'm not joking. Where are we headed?"

"Nowhere and everywhere." He glanced at the cell phone lying on the seat between them. "Pull down the center console, will you? I'll be able to see my phone better if it's in its holder," Ben said, watching her struggle to comply. "There's a release lever on your side. You have to push that in first."

"You could have told me."

"Sorry. I figured everybody knew how it worked."

Amused, Jamie lowered the console between them, then righted herself. "I hate to disillusion you, but this is the first Jeep I've ever ridden in."

"You have led a dull life, haven't you?" he joked.

"Hah!" she shot back. "As if there is anything dull about being orphaned, then marrying the wrong man and splitting from him before witnessing a murder and having to go on the run like a fugitive."

"Don't overlook the good things," Ben said. "Did you have a happy childhood? Enjoy school? Make lots of friends?"

"Yes." She knew what he was doing but it was comforting to hear him voice reminders of her happier times, so she let him continue.

"When you first got married, were you happy?"

"I thought I was."

"How about your baby? Does having her to look forward to feel joyful? You act like it."

"Of course." As was her new habit, Jamie lightly caressed the tight skin at what had once been a slim waist.

"See? You're smiling, too."

She was, wasn't she? "I get the point. I do. It's just hard to keep from worrying about the future when some lowlife thugs are trying to keep me from having one." Saying that caused her to search the mirror images again. The vehicle she had been concerned about was nowhere in sight. If there had been danger there, it was gone.

"I think we lost them or that black SUV wasn't pursuing us, after all," Ben said.

"You read my mind. That's another thing to be thankful for."

"What is? Losing the SUV or my knowing what you're thinking?"

"Losing sight of that black car," Jamie said. "I'll probably never get over jumping whenever I spot one like it."

"Nothing wrong with staying on your toes."

She glanced down at her feet. "Speaking of which, it looks like my ankles are swelling a little. My ob-gyn warned me about sitting too long. Can we stop soon and walk around a little?"

Judging by Ben's furrowed brow, the answer was *No*. Well, no worries. She'd do isometrics while they drove and make up for inaction later.

Traffic was getting heavier. The cell phone propped atop the console had been silent ever since Ben had used it, but she could see it now had a stronger signal. That was a good sign. One worth mentioning.

"Something else to be thankful for." Jamie pointed. "See?"

"Yes. I just wish somebody would tell us the new plan for you."

"New plan? What new plan?"

"I'm assuming the FBI will send a car or a chopper for you ASAP. We can only keep running for so long before the people alerted by our friend in the cabin spot us."

"I wish I hadn't asked."

"You said you wanted the truth."

"I know, I know. I did. I do. It's just…" She broke off, puzzled by why a silver pickup with dual rear tires had caught her attention as it passed going the opposite direction.

Swiveling as best she could, she tried to look directly behind them, then switched to using the side mirror. Her breath caught when she saw the larger truck making a U-turn.

"Ben!"

His knuckles whitened on the wheel. He nodded. "Yeah, I see him."

"Is he after us?"

Before Ben nodded Jamie knew the answer. She'd known the second they had passed. Something about the other vehicle had grabbed the K-9 cop's attention as well.

Worse, Shadow had stiffened and begun growling. Apparently he was picking up a sense of fear from her. And he was so right. The silver truck was gaining on them.

She looked to Ben. Saw his jaw clenching.

Felt a hard nudge from behind followed instantly by Ben's acceleration.

If she hadn't pressed her hand over her mouth at that moment she would have screamed. They'd been overtaken.

TWENTY

Ben shouted to Jamie. "Make sure your seat belt is secure but not directly over the baby."

"Can we outrun them?"

"I don't know."

Muscles flexed to the max, he stopped feeling pain in his side. Adrenaline did that in situations of elevated threat, which was what enabled people to lift cars off loved ones or run like the wind when they'd never done so before.

Thankful to see his passenger following directions, he concentrated fully on their situation. His Jeep was more maneuverable but the silver truck was heavier. How fast it was remained to be seen and he was not looking forward to finding out the hard way.

"Strapped tight?" he yelled.

"Yes! Glad I'm not driving."

"So, am I." Waiting until he'd negotiated a tight bend in the road he said, "If we go off the pavement your airbag may deploy. Cross both arms in front of your face to protect yourself."

"What about you?"

How typical of this extraordinary woman, Ben thought. She was more worried about him than she was about herself. "I'll be fine. The steering wheel will give me something to hang on to."

Or impale me, his imagination added. As he saw it, the only viable escape plan was to out-run the truck. Whether his Jeep had the neces-sary horsepower was the vital question.

Racing along the narrow highway, Ben had to slow for curves, particularly if those parts of the pavement lay in shady areas where snow and ice remained, even this late in spring. Any-one who forgot that was in for a nasty surprise, whether their vehicle had four-wheel drive or not.

Coming out of a particularly tight turn, he glanced back just in time to see the silver du-ally coming hard at him. Before he could warn Jamie, they'd been hit again. This time she yelled in fright.

"I don't know what he's got under that hood, but it's more horses than we have." Ben saw her bracing with the handhold next to her door and grabbing the edge of the console. "I'm doing my best," he shouted, discouraged that his ultimate efforts were inadequate this time.

"Here he comes again." Ben was gripping the steering wheel so hard his hands ached and his knuckles paled.

Jamie screamed the instant the heavy brush guard on the front of the silver pickup hit the left rear of their vehicle.

Ben fought to maintain control, failed and as a last resort tried to block Jamie's forward motion with his arm.

They sailed over the berm on their right and bounced once before careening down a steep incline and coming to rest in a field of boulders. Both airbags deployed. Ben's knocked him back against his seat.

Clouds of rock dust surrounded the Jeep. He turned off the engine and managed to catch enough breath to ask about his passenger. "Are you okay? Not hurt?"

Breathlessly, she answered. "I—I don't think so."

Fighting against the airbag, he opened his door. Loose dirt and gravel beneath his boots made tricky footing but he managed to work his way around to Jamie by leaning on the Jeep. Her door was buckled. He tried to muscle it open. Failed. Tried again.

Idling on the highway, about thirty yards

above, the silver pickup disgorged two men. Both looked to be of average height and weight. One was dressed in camo hunting clothing, like the prowler at the cabin had been, while the other looked decidedly preppy, polo shirt and all.

Shadow was barking warnings. Ben yanked open his rear door to release the K-9, then threw his whole weight into an effort to free Jamie.

Side windows had shattered on impact so he knew she could hear him. "Can you push?"

"I have been. It's really stuck," Jamie shouted. "I don't think I'll fit through the broken window. It's too small." Her voice cracked.

"Okay, hang on." Ben could barely hear himself think over Shadow's deep, menacing barking which was actually a good thing if it held off advances by their pursuers.

He pulled out a pocketknife and opened it. Desperate times called for desperate measures. "Cover your face and lean away from this side as much as you can," he told Jamie.

"What are you going to do?"

"Cut you out of there." The custom-made canvas top was no match for his sharp knife. He sliced an X over the place where she sat, then ripped the heavy fabric away. "Give me your hands."

"I can't get out that way either. I'll fall."

"I've got you. Trust me." There was no time for arguing or pleading. He offered both hands. "Turn around and kneel on the seat. I'll help you stand up."

"What about them?" He knew who Jamie meant.

"Right now it's a standoff with Shadow. Get up. Do it." To his relief she did roll over and kneel. Getting enough leverage to lift her when he was down at her level, however, wasn't working.

Ben circled to where the spare tire was clamped to the rear of the Jeep and climbed up on it so he'd be above her. "I can lift you now. Give me both hands."

Jamie was trying to help, he could tell, and he wasn't about to tell her how much heavier and cumbersome she was because of her condition. Not to mention unbalanced, in a physical way.

Holding tight, steadying, Ben wondered how he was going to assist her descent until she swung one leg over the edge of the cut opening and put her foot on the spare tire next to his. "I'll get off so you'll have more room," he began, intending to lay out a safe way for her to maneuver. Before he had a chance, he heard Shadow's barking increasing in intensity.

His back was to the road and he didn't dare let go of Jamie so he asked, "What's happening?"

"They're coming!" she squealed. "Get me down."

Ben jumped. Multiple shots echoed through the canyon. Urging Jamie to follow his lead, he took pains to keep his back to the shooters above. A pistol bullet fired from that far away might pass through him and still wound her but the chances of deadly injury were reduced if his body mass was in the way.

Arms around her, Ben ducked, forcing her to crouch. That was when he heard something different. Something that chilled his blood and made his hair prickle like the hackles of an angry dog. The louder boom sang and whined. Their foes had broken out a rifle.

Ben whirled. "Shadow!"

Jamie reached for his hand. "The dog's not hit. I see him. Come on."

The rifle boomed again. Ben spun around, feeling as if an unseen force had taken a baseball bat to his shin. When he looked down he saw why. There was a telltale hole punched in his jeans, and blood was oozing. Six inches higher and they'd have hit his femoral artery, giving him only minutes more to live.

Going by past experiences, Ben knew he had

only seconds left before the initial numbness faded and pain started to radiate, to incapacitate him. He swept Jamie into his arms and half ran, half limped toward the shelter of the rocks where he fell to his knees.

She turned and stared. "You're shot!"

"Yeah. Afraid so."

A sharp whistle brought the K-9 racing to join them. He dropped to the ground on command, panting and looking pleased with himself until he sniffed his partner's wound.

Ben stripped the police lanyard from around his neck, then put pressure on his leg. "Tie this just above the hole and use a stick to twist it tight."

"I don't know what you mean."

"Just tie it and get me a strong stick. I'll do the rest."

A man's voice boomed, echoing off the canyon walls. "It's over, Jamie. You're done."

Ben saw her skin pale, her eyes widen and her jaw gape. "That's him."

"Who?"

"Greg. My ex." A tear slid down her cheek. "You were right all along. He's one of them. He has to be."

Nodding, Ben helped her place the tourniquet on his leg. Logic was insisting that knowing the enemy was good—until the other man shouted more threats.

"If you think that baby will stop me, you're wrong," Greg yelled. "The only way you're getting out of here is in a body bag."

Jamie had never felt more helpless or hopeless in her entire life. "This is all my fault. If I hadn't taken the freelance job with Natasha I wouldn't have been at the murder scene in the first place."

"And if your rotten ex hadn't been mixed up in organized crime I wouldn't have a hole in my leg. Your point is?"

"When you put it that way it sounds different."

"You can't blame yourself for other people's actions, Jamie. You were trying to do the right thing when you split from him. If you'd stayed you'd have been in just as much danger. Maybe more."

"I didn't know. I promise you, Ben, I didn't know how truly evil he was."

Greg shouted again. "You saw me there with Hawkins. You had to. What were you going to do, darlin', wait until you were on the witness stand to tell the world, or were you saving it to blackmail me later?"

Jamie leaned closer to speak to Ben. "He's wrong. I didn't see him. I swear I didn't."

"I believe you. His guilty conscience is messing with his mind. It's easier to throw blame on you than to admit what he was responsible for."

Levering himself up against the rock, Ben began scanning the road and the rough land between. "Where's the other guy?"

She joined him. "I don't know. Wait. Look at Shadow." The clever K-9 was standing totally still, staring to their right as if sizing up vulnerable prey.

"I see him." Ben laced his fingers around his gun and used the rock to steady his aim. A rifle barrel emerged from a clump of sagebrush. Ben held his fire. Jamie wanted to order him to shoot but was afraid anything she said or did would distract him. She knew being injured was having a deleterious effect on Ben; she just couldn't tell how much.

Suddenly his gun barked once, ejecting the casing automatically and chambering a fresh bullet. Jamie had jumped when Ben fired. "Did you get him?"

"I think so. I don't see the rifle anymore." He sighed.

Jamie was favorably impressed by his lack of jubilation. This wasn't a TV cop show; it was real life. There was no valor in taking a life.

Greg kept shouting and cursing, calling Jamie every bad name in the book.

Ben's expression was dead sober. If he was looking for condemnation, he wasn't going to find it coming from her, she vowed. He'd only done what he'd been forced to do.

Finally, he seemed satisfied enough to manage a lopsided smile. "One down, one to go."

A bullet zinged past them. Jamie ducked lower and watched Ben return the rapid fire. The pistol action locked open.

"What's wrong? Is it jammed?" she asked, fighting panic.

"No. Out of ammo."

He ejected the empty clip, reached into the pocket of his vest and froze for a long second before starting to pat his other pockets. Color drained from his face. Sweat dotted his brow. She could only think of one reason why he'd be so distressed.

"You don't have any more bullets?" Her voice broke with emotion.

"I thought I did."

They'd been in such a rush to leave the cabin that maybe the extra clips had been left behind. "What can I do? How can I help?"

Ben was shaking his head. "I have no idea."

Huddled next to him she felt another contraction beginning. Determined to hide it to alleviate Ben's worries she held her breath, waited and felt the initial pain begin as before. Long fingers of it crept around her to clamp like a vise. Above all she must not let on. Not yet. Help was already on the way from the closest big city, Sheridan, and the K-9 unit must have relayed their plight to the FBI. Surely one or more agencies would send help soon.

When she grasped his arm and squeezed she didn't intend to hurt him. All she wanted, needed, was moral support. As her grip tightened she found herself unable to release him. Her eyes were filling with tears and although she did manage to bite them back she wasn't able to stifle a cry.

Despite the pain from his wounds Ben locked eyes with her. "Are you…?"

Nodding, she had to be truthful, "Yes."

"How long?"

"At first I thought it was another false alarm. But then…" Stepping back slightly she pointed at the damp ground. "I guess it's real this time. It sure feels real."

The pathos in his dark eyes was so evident Jamie almost wept. "I'm so sorry, Ben."

He took her hand gently. "No. I'm the one who's sorry. I got you into this."

"Don't be ridiculous. That's my ex out there

cursing his head off. If he wasn't such a coward he'd have walked up and shot me already."

"Us, you mean. We're in this together."

"I'd offer to give myself up if I wasn't carrying this baby," Jamie said. "I just can't quit on her."

"Of course you can't."

The contraction had ended, leaving her panting from the effort of trying to control herself. Weary and despondent she wrapped her arms around Ben's waist and laid her head on his shoulder.

Wind had increased and was picking up sand and grit that stung like tiny needles. Peeking out, Jamie saw Greg swiping at his eyes.

He was also cautiously working his way closer.

And he was armed.

TWENTY-ONE

Ben was certain Shadow could take down any shooter, but there was no guarantee the brave K-9 wouldn't be hurt or killed doing it. Ideally, he, as Shadow's partner, would provide armed backup and handcuff the prisoner as soon as the dog subdued him. That promised to be tricky to do with sore ribs, a bullet hole in his leg and an empty gun. The harsh wind, however, helped to even the playing field by making it hard for their assailant to see clearly.

"Look, you stay here," Ben told Jamie. He'd grasped her upper arms to set her away and bent down until they were practically nose to nose. "I have an idea."

Her grip on his vest was viselike. "No. You're already wounded. We do this together."

"Humph." A glance up and down her body was intended to make his point.

Apparently it did because she began to sniffle. "I can help some way. I know I can. How about a distraction?"

"Shadow won't need help until he gets Greg on the ground. It's normally up to me to disarm a suspect, and I will, it just might take me longer than usual to get there and take control."

"Do you want *me* to do that?"

"Absolutely not."

"Then what?" This time she had two fistfuls of his vest and her grip was tightening.

"You're in labor. Isn't that enough to keep you occupied?" Ben had to give her credit for courage. "Can you walk?"

"Of course I can. The only time I'm incapacitated is during a contraction."

"How often are you having those?"

"I don't know. They aren't regular like I thought they'd be. Does it usually take your heifers longer for the first calf?"

Ben was incredulous. "You're asking me for birthing advice?" Movement had ceased on the slope where Greg had been, which would have pleased Ben if he could see where the armed man had gone. Looking to Shadow and following the K-9's gaze, he pinpointed their attacker's hiding place. It was too close for comfort. Time was not on their side but at least Greg wasn't running at them, firing randomly.

"Okay." Pulling Jamie closer, Ben whispered

so his plan wouldn't be overheard. "When I send Shadow to attack I'll be right behind him. As soon as Greg is disarmed I want you to see if you can find my phone in the Jeep."

"Why?"

"So I can order an ambulance and get an ETA." *If I'm still conscious*, he added to himself. "Or you can if I'm sitting on your ex."

"Right. Got it. Oops."

Ben saw her catch her breath and hold it. "Another one?"

"I thought so, but it didn't amount to much."

"You good to go now?"

"Give me a sec."

To Ben's surprise it was easier for him to read Jamie's expressions than those of folks he'd known all his life. It was as though their shared trauma had connected them somehow. One thing he knew for certain. He was more than ready to give his all for her—and for a baby no one had ever seen.

As soon as Jamie squared her shoulders and nodded, he directed his full attention to Shadow. The faithful K-9 was quivering all over, bracing for the command he was about to receive, as if intuitively knowing his human partner's thoughts.

Ben stepped away from Jamie, paused for a moment to battle dizziness, then raised one hand and gave his dog the command to attack. "Take hold!"

Shadow took off like a sprinter leaving the starting blocks in the most important race of his life.

Teeth gritted, fists clenched, Ben was right behind him.

Watching both her human and canine companions charging directly into danger brought Jamie up short. She couldn't take her eyes off them, either of them. The dog pulled farther and farther ahead while Ben struggled along with a half-hopping gait. How difficult it must be to push himself forward through a haze of pain. And speaking of pain...

Temporarily clear of discomfort, apart from a heaviness in her pelvis that she hadn't noticed before, Jamie headed for the wrecked Jeep. It had occurred to her that Ben might have given her this task as a way to keep her busy while he tended to business. That was okay. The mere notion that she might be helping was enough, particularly because she couldn't imagine how they were going to get out of this current mess in one piece.

The analogy was almost enough to make her smile. Time was coming soon when she and her daughter would become two separate individuals. At this point, Jamie wasn't sure whether she was prepared for full-blown labor but that was no longer up to her, was it? Truth to tell, it never had been. For reasons known only to God, He had given her a child. She'd prayed for rescue from a bad marriage and He had not only let her see a life taken, He was about to show her a life's renewal.

A shout from Ben sent a shiver up her spine. Shadow was barking and growling loudly enough to be heard over the pulse thudding in her ears. Still, that meant that her defenders were having success. She took a deep breath and climbed the last few paces to the Jeep, then leaned against it, panting from exertion and fear.

About to open the driver's-side door she heard a single gunshot. Every nerve in her body fired. And she promptly had another contraction.

Ben was in time to see Greg fire wildly when Shadow jumped him. The brave dog never flinched. Chances were that even with an injury the K-9 would bite, and bite he did.

Greg was knocked back. Shadow bit the arm holding the gun and held on, shaking the mouthful of assailant the way a wolf would shake its prey while the man beat on him with his free arm and fist.

Ben threw himself into the fray. Once he was off his feet he was able to better concentrate on subduing the punishing blows to Shadow.

"He's breaking my wrist!" Greg screeched at the top of his lungs.

"He'll take off your hand if you don't let go of that gun," Ben shouted over the growling and shrieking. "Drop it. Now."

"Okay, okay."

At this point Ben realized he had an additional problem. He'd used up the zip ties he'd carried on the prowler at the cabin. All he could do was sit on Greg and let Shadow continue to hold him down until help arrived. Or until he passed out from shock and loss of blood, he added with chagrin. There was no excuse for the mess he was in. None. A seasoned cop and army ranger was supposed to have his act together.

The main problem was Jamie London, Ben admitted. She was not only a distraction, he'd let himself care too much. That kind of error was bound to hamper clear thinking. And now she was having her baby out in the middle of nowhere while he bled into unconsciousness and his K-9 was the only one still properly focused. Ironic didn't even begin to describe the situation.

Readying for renewed resistance, Ben commanded, "Release," followed immediately by pointing and saying, "Gun". The hero dog carefully picked it up and delivered it to hand.

"Good boy." Ben eased away from the man on the ground while Greg cradled his bitten, bleeding wrist, rolled from side to side and moaned.

Sufficiently far enough away to avoid a lunge, should one come, Ben propped himself up, aimed the captured gun at his prisoner and said, "Try anything and I'll send the dog again."

From the looks of Greg Jennings, he wasn't going to cause further trouble, which would have been a bigger relief if Ben hadn't had Jamie to worry about. He was about to yell to her, to urge her to join him, when he felt a rhythmic vibration in the air. A solid black chopper rose over the ridge, its prop wash driving grit in all directions like needles. Ben didn't care how much his skin stung. Backup had arrived.

Now all they had to do was figure out how to land in territory rougher than the surface of the moon.

Jamie'd had to stop twice on her way back to Ben. Until she saw him for herself she wasn't going to be satisfied so she'd tried to carry the loaded shotgun from the Jeep. By the end of the second contraction she'd stashed the heavy weapon and proceeded with only the cell phone.

The moment she laid eyes on her cowboy cop her heart leaped with joy and her body sagged in relief. He had the drop on Greg, and Shadow was standing guard like a starving lion hovering over its next meal. That sight renewed her energy beyond imagining. So did the arrival of a helicopter.

Ducking and pulling the hood of her coat over her head she worked her way through the dust cloud to Ben. "You did it!"

"Shadow did. I just helped."

Thankfully, the chopper's altitude was rising so they could hear each other. "Who cares?" The urge to throw her arms around his neck was strong, but she knew better than to cause a distraction. Instead, she reached into her pocket and found a leftover zip tie which she offered as if it was a precious gift. "Want this?"

"You're amazing," Ben told her. "Will you do the honors?"

"I'd love to." No longer afraid of the pitiful-looking man lying in the dirt groaning, she approached. "Stick out your hands."

"I'm dying here, Jamie. You can't tie me up. That stupid dog broke my wrist."

All the added incentive she needed came from a glance at Ben and the signal of his lifted chin. She couldn't smile but she did sense closure of a painful part of her life.

"No, he didn't. Let me put this tie on you or I'll tell Shadow to chew up the other side." She wouldn't, of course, even if she'd been able to, but Greg didn't need to know that.

Before ratcheting the plastic tie tight she paused to check his bite injury, then pulled down the cuff of his sleeve, holding it in place with the tie as a temporary bandage. Anybody, even as evil a man as this, deserved that much courtesy.

"Why did you think I saw you at the murder scene?" she asked her ex. "Hawkins was the one standing over Natasha with a gun."

Greg coughed. Grimaced. "Don't lie. Not now. I was there and you know it."

If he had been there, she hadn't seen him. "You ordered Hawkins to kill Natasha because you wanted to hide your affair?"

This time his cough morphed into a laugh. "Affair? Hah! You're no brighter than she was. I never cared about her. All I wanted to do was find out how much she knew. She thought she was going to trick me into revealing the name of the boss of the drug-trafficking ring. I was pumping her for information, instead. Once she tumbled to the truth we didn't need her anymore."

Blinking back unshed tears, Jamie looked to Ben. "Should you read him his rights?"

Instead of a reply she saw his hand shaking, his eyes struggling to focus. He partially raised the captured pistol. "Take this and aim it at him. I think I hear sirens."

Jamie started to comply, then doubled over, instead. "I sure hope so because this contraction hurts a lot more than the other ones did."

To her relief, Ben seemed to rally. "Okay. I've got this. Sit down before you fall down."

"You should talk," she countered. "Oh, ow."

"Come over here by me," Ben urged. "You can help me hold the gun up when you're not busy having that baby."

As soon as she felt steady again she lowered herself to the ground beside him. "Nice of you to share."

"Anything for you, honey."

"What did you just call me?"

Ben was smiling. "I can't be held responsible for anything I say. I'm probably in shock."

"So am I," Jamie said, leaning on his shoulder. "We really should talk."

"Later," Ben said as he slipped his free arm around her. "Here comes the cavalry."

Paramedics had parked on the road along with at least one police car that she could see. Jamie held up his cell phone. "I forgot to tell you. I used your speed dial to call your boss and ask for an ambulance."

"If you ever decide to give up photography you should consider becoming a cop."

"No thanks," she said, snuggling closer and silently thanking God for their deliverance, even if it had come at the last possible minute. In her mind, as she replayed his compliment, more words followed that sent her heart racing. What she wanted to say, wanted to tell him, was, *One cop in the family is enough.*

That unbidden conclusion should have startled her. It didn't until she realized she was okay with it. Had facing possible death and defeating it drawn them that close? Was it possible to set aside months of sensible decisions in the space of barely a week? Logic said no.

Jamie gazed up at Ben's scruffy cheek and realized, without a doubt, that her heart was saying yes. She loved him in spite of everything.

Her first reaction to that conclusion was a smile. Her second was a murmured, "Oh, dear."

TWENTY-TWO

Ben insisted that the medics care for Jamie first and she objected, just as he'd figured she would, until another contraction changed her mind. He offered to let her be transported to the hospital alone in spite of yearning to stay with her. It was a relief when the decision was made to take them to Sheridan together in the ambulance and send Greg to ER in the back of a patrol car.

"What about my K-9?" Ben asked. "He's an official police officer assigned to work with me. Plus, he saved us from ending up dead. Don't you think he deserves to go along?"

"Not in our sterile ambulance," one of the paramedics said.

A nearby state trooper spoke up. "I can give him a lift as long as he doesn't bite me."

"Open the door of your unit and stand back," Ben said, rising from the gurney on an elbow and pointing as soon as the trooper complied. "Shadow. Car."

The Doberman cocked his head to the side as if questioning the order. Ben nodded. "Yes. Car. Get in."

In seconds, the intelligent K-9 was seated in the passenger seat and acting as if he always rode shotgun for strange police officers.

"Good boy," Ben said, smiling.

After delaying only a moment to tell the trooper where to find Shadow's leash and working vest in the Jeep, Ben laid back down. Man, he was beat. Between the peaks of adrenaline, being shot and his witness going into labor it had been a roller coaster morning.

Jamie rested across the narrow aisle on a similar gurney while they traveled. A different medic monitored her vital signs. Thankfully, she didn't look nearly as bad as he felt, Ben mused. That was a good sign. A bright white sheet covered her and he saw her gather fists full of it when another contraction came.

Because he was strapped down he could reach out with only one arm. Straining to span the aisle he said, "Here. Take my hand."

"You may be sorry," she warned. "This baby isn't fooling around anymore."

"Neither am I." Ben had been given a mild painkiller before the other medic had cut away the lower leg of his jeans and begun to treat his bullet wound, so he was no longer feeling as much discomfort.

"I'm so glad you're here," Jamie said. Tears trickled from the corners of her eyes as she turned her head to give him a wan smile. "It's nice to have somebody."

"You mean somebody who cares about you and the baby, right?"

"Yes." Sniffling, she nodded.

"I do, you know." He gave her fingers a tender squeeze. "I suppose this isn't the right time or place but I want you to know how special I think you are."

"You hardly know me."

He had to agree. "Yeah. I've been telling myself the same thing over and over and it still seems like we've known each other for ages."

"It does, doesn't it? I wonder why."

"I have no idea except to chalk it up to divine providence. If you and I had met under any other circumstances we might not have dropped our guards enough to even get acquainted."

"You, too?" Jamie asked. "I'd sworn off relationships because of Greg. Why would you have been put off?"

"My history. My dysfunctional family. All I know is, the notion of becoming a father has suddenly stopped giving me cold sweats."

"How romantic." A soft laugh was interrupted by a tightening of her whole body and a grip on his hand that was punishing in its intensity.

Ben stopped talking and waited for her pain to pass. "I don't want to make my father's mistakes. Dad will pay the rest of his life for the way he and his family treated my half brother's mom. I can see why he made the choices he did but that doesn't erase the consequences."

Jamie had an IV in her other arm, so she let the medic mop perspiration from her brow. "Mistakes are my specialty. Even when I remember to pray first I still make them." She looked at the sheet that was draped over her bent knees and sighed. "I hope we get to the hospital in time."

"What happened to my pioneer wife, bravely having babies on the seat of a covered wagon?"

"She was out of her mind," Jamie snapped back. She frowned over at him. "Wait a second. What wife?"

"Ah, well, I am currently drugged so maybe that's why it's so easy to tell you I love you. I think we should get married."

"You do?"

"Yes."

Pain made him grit his teeth and empathy

cleared the last obstacles to Jamie admitting the same feelings. "I love you, too, Ben."

He blew a sigh. "Glad that's settled. I've been thinking. If you need a good place to recover after the baby is born you can't do better than the Double S. I can get Mrs. Edgerton to stay with you until you're back on your feet. She can help you take care of..." Ben broke off. "She really needs a name. You'll have to choose soon."

"My mother's name was June."

Ben smiled at her. "Good choice."

"I think so. Keep it in the family." Jamie's tender smile spread, and her green eyes glistened like leafy trees after a spring shower.

He thought he had control of his thoughts and emotions until Jamie said, "I'm going to call her Barbara June, after your mother and mine."

Only bits and pieces of the rest of that day were with Jamie the following morning. A couple of things had stuck in her mind, things she was pretty sure she'd never forget.

Of course, there was the dash to escape, the crash, getting cut out of the Jeep with a pocketknife and Ben's bullet wound. Those were certainly memorable. So was watching Shadow take down Greg and disarm him. If she was called upon to testify about his impromptu confession she was going to do so gladly.

The most unforgettable event of the day, however, other than the eventual birth of Barbara June, was the expression on Ben's dear face when she'd told him the baby's name was going to be Barbara. He didn't sob. He simply kept looking at her with an expression of unspoken love as tears streamed down his face and dampened the pillow beneath his head. To her, he had never looked more handsome or more wonderful.

That was what she was thinking about when there was a tapping at her door. *Ben?* Had he come to see her?

"I have your baby, Ms. London," a nurse said. "Would you like to hold her?"

Jamie could only nod. She'd been able to see and comfort Barbara June right after she was born but hadn't seen her since.

The warm bundle of tightly wrapped receiving blankets seemed so tiny, so fragile, Jamie was almost afraid to hold her.

"She won't break," the nurse said pleasantly. "I'll be back in about thirty minutes. You take the time to get to know your daughter."

On the way out, the nurse paused in the doorway and leaned back around to ask, "Are you up to having visitors?"

"I guess so." The only person Jamie could think of was Ben so when the Edgertons peeked in she had to work to cover disappointment. "Hello."

"Hi, sweetie," Mrs. E said while her husband stood back and grinned. "I didn't know what you'd gathered for a layette so I went out and picked up a few things. Oh, and we'd be glad to loan you the crib I used to raise my three if my daughter-in-law wasn't already using it. I brought your laptop in case you want to order things online and have them delivered to the ranch."

"Am I going there? Really? I was afraid it was all a dream." She cradled the baby like a doll, noticing how sweet and wonderful she smelled.

"No dream. I'll take care of everything, get you whatever you need and be ready to rock that little one whenever you need a nap."

"I have a date in court in Denver at the end of this month. They want me to testify that I saw Hawkins holding the gun even though Greg has admitted firing the initial shot, then sending his flunky back to finish the job."

"We'll be ready whenever you are. No problem."

"How is Ben? Have you seen him?"

"We just left his room. He was arguin' with a nurse about gettin' up and comin' to see you. Not sure who was gonna win."

"I did," Ben said from the open doorway. On crutches and favoring a bandaged calf below cutoff green surgical pants and a matching top, he was as dressed as he could probably get under these circumstances.

Jamie forgot everyone but him. The glow on his face could be joy or embarrassment or caused by the exertion of getting to her. She didn't care. He was here. That was all that mattered.

She displayed her daughter. "Look."

"Beautiful. Like her mother."

"Well, sit down, sit down," the older woman urged, scooting a chair across the vinyl-tiled floor and positioning it behind him next to the bed. "You can't hold her standing up like that."

Jamie might not have relinquished the baby to anyone else, but this was Ben. *Her* Ben, if things worked out the way she'd been praying they would.

He plunked down, laid aside the crutches and held out his hands. As Jamie placed the tiny human in Ben's loving arms the sight banished all doubt. Both were new additions to her life and both already so dear the sight of them stole her breath away. It didn't matter how long she and Ben waited or if they decided to get married soon. Nothing was going to make her change her mind. Nothing was going to split them up.

Who cared how they had met and fallen in love? It was a done deal. They were a couple. A family.

She smiled at Ben while he was smiling at baby Barbara. They already had it all, even the family dog, in a manner of speaking. Uh-oh. Would Shadow be okay around the baby?

"Shadow," Jamie began, "will he be jealous?"

"Nope." Ben's eyes were shining. "He's been trained to tolerate all sizes of people, even itty-bitty ones like this."

Relief washed over her. This was going to work. This was really going to work. And the beauty of that blessing was so overwhelming all she could do was grin at Ben and thank God for bringing them together.

When she whispered, "Thank you, Jesus," Ben added, "Amen."

EPILOGUE

To Jamie's relief and delight, Ben was waiting for her outside the courthouse when she finished testifying and greeted her by grinning and slipping an arm around her shoulders.

She leaned in, drawing strength. "Thanks. It's been a long day, even if our doctors did okay it for both of us."

"I'll take it easy driving you back home to the ranch."

"No more sliding around corners and flying through the air? Good." How wonderful it was to picture the Double S as home. A perfect place to honeymoon as soon as possible.

"Your time on the stand didn't take long," Ben said, adding a quick hug.

"Really? It seemed like forever."

He laughed tenderly. "I imagine you didn't hear all the interesting details while you were in the courtroom, but I've talked to an assistant DA. I can fill you in if you want."

"Anything, as long as we can leave Denver for the time being and finish recuperating at the ranch."

"Promise." They started to thread through the crowd, heading for the exit. "The charge against William Hawkins has been reduced to accessory to murder because he's agreed to testify against Greg."

"Really? Greg was the shooter."

"Yes. The most important charges against Jennings include the murder of Congresswoman Clark and the attempted murder of you and me. Money laundering comes in a poor third."

"I'm glad the guy you had to shoot by the Jeep didn't die. Is he going to be okay?"

"More than okay. He's agreed to give testimony and so has the man we left tied up at the cabin. Greg is finished."

"I'm so relieved. Did the FBI learn anything new from my pictures of Natasha's fundraiser?"

"Boy, did they. Hawkins was right there in the background, for one thing. And it turns out good old Greg was wrong about taking advantage of her. He was being played himself. Natasha Clark was up to her eyeballs in the same criminal syndicate her committee was pretending to investigate. If your ex hadn't killed her she might have done a lot more damage than she already had."

"Wow. Talk about getting justice the hard way." Thinking about her newborn, she recalled one of Ben's prior concerns. "Speaking of justice, have you guys located that missing baby whose mother was found dead in her car in the ravine? I feel so sorry for the poor little thing."

"Chloe Baker. No. We hope to get answers from Kate Montgomery, but she's still in a coma. Chloe's car seat and baby blanket were found near Kate's body, so we think the baby was traveling with her, but we don't know why the two women were targeted. We won't give up on finding Chloe. I promise you," he said soberly. "But we don't solve every crime no matter how hard we try."

Jamie took a deep breath. So much trauma, so many hurting people. And always the chance of danger to Ben and others trying to help. She leaned in to him and closed her eyes. "Sorry. I'm exhausted. It was a rough week even before I had to face Greg in court," she said, hoping to feel Ben's strong arms close around her.

Instead, he stepped away. "I was going to wait until we got home, but I want to make it official. I think you need a piece of my heart close to you as soon as possible." He produced a royal blue ring box and opened it. "Will you marry me, Jamie London?"

When she didn't immediately say yes, he continued. "I'll get down on one knee if that's what it takes, no matter how much my leg hurts."

Smiling, she cupped her hands around his. "You want both of us? You're sure?"

"Positive."

"Then yes. I'll marry you. I love you, Ben Sawyer."

He was grinning and sliding the sparkling diamond engagement ring on her finger when they were joined by two other members of his K-9 unit. Both were wearing their RMKU badges on lanyards around their necks just as Ben was. She recognized his boss, Tyson Wilkes. The other man didn't seem particularly amiable.

"First Nelson and Mia get married in a New York minute and now the two of you are engaged. I hope it's not contagious," Tyson said, shaking Ben's hand rigorously. "Looks like congratulations are in order."

"Thanks," Ben said. "You know Jamie but Chris doesn't." Ben turned to face the second man. "Chris, I'd like you to meet Jamie London. Jamie, this is my brother, Chris Fuller, the one I told you about."

Hoping she didn't show surprise, she offered her hand just as Ben had. "Pleased to meet you."

While Chris was tentatively shaking her right hand, Jamie laid her left over their clasped hands and prayed he'd understand the meaning of the magnanimous gesture. She wanted this man to feel accepted by every member of her new extended family, and if he was willing to start with her, that would be one of the best gifts she could possibly give her future husband.

Ben didn't say a word. He didn't have to. Jamie could see love and approval sparkling more brightly in his eyes than the diamond token he'd just placed on her finger.

He hadn't pressed her to set a date for their marriage but it was going to be soon. Very soon. Under a blue Wyoming sky and attended by all of Ben's family members.

A grin spread across her face as she mentally added one more detail. Shadow would make the perfect ring-bearer.

* * * * *

Don't miss Ben's brother Chris's story,
Hiding in Montana, *and the rest of the*
Rocky Mountain K-9 Unit series:

Detection Detail *by Terri Reed,*
April 2022

Ready to Protect *by Valerie Hansen,*
May 2022

Hiding in Montana *by Laura Scott,*
June 2022

Undercover Assignment *by Dana Mentink,*
July 2022

Defending from Danger *by Jodie Bailey,*
August 2022

Tracking a Killer *by Elizabeth Goddard,*
September 2022

Explosive Revenge *by Maggie K. Black,*
October 2022

Rescue Mission *by Lynette Eason,*
November 2022

Christmas K-9 Unit Heroes
by Lenora Worth and Katy Lee,
December 2022

Dear Reader,

People who choose to do the right thing are heroes. Those who stand behind them and support their efforts are, too, even if they happen to be K-9s. When we think of dogs most of us tend to see them as pets, but they are much more. They are friends, allies and protectors who bring joy with their antics yet comfort us in trials and stand by us at perhaps our lowest moments. They locate lost children and adults. They bark at predators for shepherds and delivery men for city dwellers. They intuitively know what their special humans need and give all they have no matter what it costs them.

I have a funny T-shirt that says, "Lord, Please Help Me Become the Wonderful Person My Dog Thinks I Am." That pretty much says it all.

I can be reached best by email—val@valeriehansen.com and my website is www.ValerieHansen.com. Antics and updates on me are posted on Facebook—https:/www.facebook.com/Valerie.Whisenand.

Be blessed. God loves you,

Valerie Hansen

Get 4 FREE REWARDS!

We'll send you 2 FREE Books plus 2 FREE Mystery Gifts.

FREE
Value Over
$20

Both the **Love Inspired®** and **Love Inspired® Suspense** series feature compelling novels filled with inspirational romance, faith, forgiveness, and hope.

YES! Please send me 2 FREE novels from the Love Inspired or Love Inspired Suspense series and my 2 FREE gifts (gifts are worth about $10 retail). After receiving them, if I don't wish to receive any more books, I can return the shipping statement marked "cancel." If I don't cancel, I will receive 6 brand-new Love Inspired Larger-Print books or Love Inspired Suspense Larger-Print books every month and be billed just $5.99 each in the U.S. or $6.24 each in Canada. That is a savings of at least 17% off the cover price. It's quite a bargain! Shipping and handling is just 50¢ per book in the U.S. and $1.25 per book in Canada.* I understand that accepting the 2 free books and gifts places me under no obligation to buy anything. I can always return a shipment and cancel at any time. The free books and gifts are mine to keep no matter what I decide.

Choose one: ☐ **Love Inspired**
Larger-Print
(122/322 IDN GNWC)

☐ **Love Inspired Suspense**
Larger-Print
(107/307 IDN GNWN)

Name (please print)

Address   Apt. #

City   State/Province   Zip/Postal Code

Email: Please check this box ☐ if you would like to receive newsletters and promotional emails from Harlequin Enterprises ULC and its affiliates. You can unsubscribe anytime.

Mail to the Harlequin Reader Service:
IN U.S.A.: P.O. Box 1341, Buffalo, NY 14240-8531
IN CANADA: P.O. Box 603, Fort Erie, Ontario L2A 5X3

Want to try 2 free books from another series! Call 1-800-873-8635 or visit www.ReaderService.com.

---

*Terms and prices subject to change without notice. Prices do not include sales taxes, which will be charged (if applicable) based on your state or country of residence. Canadian residents will be charged applicable taxes. Offer not valid in Quebec. This offer is limited to one order per household. Books received may not be as shown. Not valid for current subscribers to the Love Inspired or Love Inspired Suspense series. All orders subject to approval. Credit or debit balances in a customer's account(s) may be offset by any other outstanding balance owed by or to the customer. Please allow 4 to 6 weeks for delivery. Offer available while quantities last.

Your Privacy—Your information is being collected by Harlequin Enterprises ULC, operating as Harlequin Reader Service. For a complete summary of the information we collect, how we use this information and to whom it is disclosed, please visit our privacy notice located at corporate.harlequin.com/privacy-notice. From time to time we may also exchange your personal information with reputable third parties. If you wish to opt out of this sharing of your personal information, please visit readerservice.com/consumerschoice or call 1-800-873-8635. **Notice to California Residents**—Under California law, you have specific rights to control and access your data. For more information on these rights and how to exercise them, visit corporate.harlequin.com/california-privacy.

LIRLIS22

Get 4 FREE REWARDS!

We'll send you 2 FREE Books _plus_ 2 FREE Mystery Gifts.

FREE Value Over **$20**

Both the **Worldwide Library** and **Essential Suspense** series feature compelling novels filled with gripping mysteries, edge of your seat thrillers and heart-stopping romantic suspense stories.

Visit ReaderService.com Today!

As a valued member of the Harlequin Reader Service, you'll find these benefits and more at ReaderService.com:

- Try 2 free books from any series
- Access risk-free special offers
- View your account history & manage payments
- Browse the latest Bonus Bucks catalog

Don't miss out!

If you want to stay up-to-date on the latest at the Harlequin Reader Service and enjoy more content, make sure you've signed up for our monthly News & Notes email newsletter. Sign up online at ReaderService.com or by calling Customer Service at 1-800-873-8635.